WIFE NOT REQUIRED

C. C. COLDWELL

Cover by Carpe Librum Book Design
www.carpelibrumbookdesign.com

To Clara, Cathryn and Jason.

CHAPTER ONE

The Dakota Territory

Spring, 1868

The train's low, haunting whistle pierced through the quiet prairie before spewing one last cloud of black smoke and pulling away from the platform. Matilda Robinson watched it disappear into a small dot on the landscape then took a breath and turned anxiously to glance around at her new home.

The small town of Boxwood was nothing like New York City, Mattie thought happily. She'd never been anywhere so new, so unhurried, so peaceful. A strand of unruly brown hair escaped its thick braid and darted across her face, blown by the fresh spring wind. She smoothed it back into place and adjusted her hat as best she could without a mirror. Boxwood's train station was nothing more than a platform of roughly sawn logs beside a muddy and rutted main street but Mattie thought the whole town had promise. There was already a small two-story hotel and a general store, a bank, and a telegraph office. As if to convince her of its newness, every so often Mattie caught the scent of fresh sawdust waft through the air from a construction site beside the telegraph office. Yes, she decided. This town held promise and if the town held promise then maybe her marriage held promise as well.

Mattie opened her reticule and took out her husband's tintype and letter. She examined John Stark's picture for the hundredth time since boarding the train in New York City. *He looks strong and dependable,* she thought. His eyes seemed kind and she supposed his mustache was distinguished, though a little bit longer than the fashion in New York. Mattie didn't even mind that he was nearly thirty years her senior. Many couples had large age differences, she reasoned. She was hopeful that in time mutual respect could grow between them and they would come to care for each other.

And what would he think of her, Mattie wondered. She looked down at the large, rough hands holding the tintype, hands that fittingly matched her six-foot-tall, sturdy frame. She remembered some of the neighborhood boys who had taunted her, telling her she was built like a bulldog with a face to match. As she matured into a young woman, she found that many women were just as cruel only their barbs

WIFE NOT REQUIRED

were concealed as concern and sympathy. They patted her hand and lamented over the fact that she was so tall, helpfully suggested what clothing to wear to make her appear slimmer and advised her to try skipping a few meals.

She quickly shut out those painful memories. Annoyed at herself for indulging in self-pity, Mattie sat up a little straighter and tried to look cheerful and confident. She was smart and quick, resourceful and a good conversationalist, or so she'd been told by the few men who had courted her briefly over her twenty-six years. She just hoped that Mr. Stark wouldn't be too disappointed. Mattie smoothed and straightened her tan traveling suit then nervously sat down on her trunk. She glanced across the street to the clock on the front of the bank building and frowned. She'd sent a telegram from Chicago with her expected date and time of arrival in Boxwood and the train had been on time. Mr. Stark had no doubt been waylaid by the many important duties on his farm, she decided. She'd waited nearly a year to meet him; she could wait a few more minutes.

Shouting at the horses, Thomas Langley angrily tried to push the wagon wheel forward through the shallow puddle. The wagon jerked forward slightly then stopped, sinking deeper into the thick Dakota mud. Letting out a cry of rage he kicked the wheel. A sharp jolt of pain shot up his right leg, into his knee and settled with a dull ache in the torn and mottled flesh on his hip. He slammed a fist into the buckboard and cursed aloud. Women were nothing but a bother.

An unsettled and dangerous land like the Dakota Territory was no place for a woman. That's exactly what he told Johnny Stark when the old fool told him he planned to send for a mail-order bride. From New York City, of all places! She'd be a useless burden and nothing but a bother. Thomas hadn't even met her and she was already an inconvenience. He was losing half a day's work to drive into town and meet the damn woman. He had fields that needed tending to, a kitchen garden that was overrun with weeds, repairs on the barn and an ornery goat that kept escaping and eating everything in sight, including the laundry hanging on the line. He didn't have time to meet with Miss Matilda Robinson.

Matilda. He rolled his eyes. The name said it all. She was no doubt a frail, pious old spinster with a pinched face and dull eyes who would bemoan the fact that there wasn't anywhere to get a decent cup of tea in Boxwood. He could just imagine her stomping a delicate little foot when she discovered that she'd have to send to Chicago for a new hat and giving him a prudish look when she found out she'd have to expose her ankles while crossing the street to keep her fine silk gown from dragging in the mud. Thomas laughed bitterly. Oh, he knew the type alright. Constantly complaining, oblivious to the dangers in the Territory, ignorant to the back-breaking work it took to survive in the west.

Resigned to his task, Thomas stomped back into the muddy water and this time leaned forward, carefully putting his shoulder to the wheel. He yelled again to the horses hitched to the wagon and pushed. The wagon lurched forward and Thomas lost his footing in the mud. He pitched forward and slammed into the side of the wagon. A strangled cry escaped his lips as he clutched at his throbbing shoulder. What did a man Johnny's age want with a wife anyway, Thomas grumbled. The old fool had managed the better part of seventy years without a wife, why did he want one now?

The clock on the bank building struck ten o'clock. Mattie looked about uneasily. What if John Stark didn't arrive? What would she do? She stood and took a deep breath. Dr. Preston's sister, Dora, lived in Boxwood. In fact, she was the one who had sent John's letter on to her brother in New York City asking for help in finding him a wife. Mattie had just made up her mind to ask after Dora at the hotel when a large figure appeared at the end of the train platform. Her stomach churned and flipped but she forced herself to stand up taller and smile.

Mattie thought at first that it was a trick of the eye, nothing more than the angle of the man's long, lean body set against the simple blue background of the Dakota sky that made him appear so tall but as he approached she realized he dwarfed her nearly six-foot-tall frame. His heavy boots stomped across the train platform in three strides, the slight limp in his right leg nearly imperceptible. His light brown hair was graying at the temples and hung long enough at the sides to cover his ears. Several deep scars, lighter in color than his tanned skin crossed his jaw and right eye. Standing in front of her, he reached up a well-muscled arm and briefly touched his hat before resting both hands on his hips. Cold grey eyes surveyed her leisurely from head to toe.

"Mr. Stark?" Mattie asked hesitantly.

"John Stark's dead," he growled.

CHAPTER TWO

"I beg your pardon, sir?" Mattie said.

"You heard me. John Stark is dead," Thomas repeated in a rough, low, southern drawl.

"There must be some mistake. I have a letter. We're to be married. He's expecting me," she finished quietly. Mattie shook her head. "I must speak to Miss Dora Preston at once. Would you be so kind as to escort me, Mr…"

"Langley. Thomas Langley," he answered. "Woman, I haven't the time nor the desire to escort you all over town. I assure you there's no mistake. John Stark died last fall of lung fever. I buried him myself. There should be another train heading east in a few days. Get on it and go back to New York City."

Mattie squared her shoulders and eyed Thomas coldly. "Very well, Mr. Langley. I shall find Miss Preston myself.

Good day." Turning on a heel, she marched down the platform toward the hotel, shoulders back and staring straight ahead. *What a rude man*, Mattie fumed. She would find Miss Preston and sort this out. There was obviously some mistake. Doctor Preston received a letter from his sister last December requesting a bride for Mr. Stark. Mattie had only taken a week to mull the matter over before writing him to say that she would arrive in Dakota Territory in early spring. Mr. Stark sent her a train ticket almost immediately. She sent several telegrams along the way, informing Mr. Stark of her progress west. Mr. Langley was obviously mistaken or perhaps he was unhinged. She shuddered. The newspapers back east were full of shocking stories of settlers succumbing to delirium, sometimes committing horrifying acts of violence. Wary of the heavy footsteps following her, Mattie stood even straighter and hastened her pace across the muddy street to the hotel.

She wrenched open the door to the hotel and entered, wiping her boots on the carpet. A young man with spectacles and wearing a tidy suit smiled at her from behind the counter.

"Good morning, ma'am," he nodded.

Mattie smiled. "Good morning. Would you be so kind as to tell me where I might find Miss Dora Preston? I am Miss Robinson from New York City and she expecting me."

The clerk frowned and shook his head. "Can't say as I know a Miss Preston. And I know just about everybody in town."

Mattie reached out and clung onto the counter. Panic rose from her stomach to her throat. Everything had been so perfectly planned and now it all seemed to be going awry so quickly.

Mattie heard the door to the hotel open and slam shut behind her. The young clerk swallowed and stood up straighter as if to make himself look taller. "Help you, sir?" he said, all trace of the friendliness he'd shown toward Mattie gone.

"She's looking for Dora Bradshaw," Thomas snarled.

"Sheriff Bradshaw's wife?" the young man said. He turned to Mattie. "She and the Sheriff are at an Indian settlement about sixty miles west of here. Won't be back for another week at least. Sheriff heard the whole reservation was stricken with fever so he and the missus packed up a bunch of supplies and headed out yesterday."

Mattie forced herself to stay calm. "Then perhaps you could help me locate Mr. John Stark?"

The clerk's face brightened. "I know exactly where Old Johnny is."

Mattie turned to Thomas and smiled. "Wonderful. I know for sure that he is expecting me. I am his betrothed."

The young man's bright smile suddenly turned downcast. "Well, ma'am. I am sorry to be the bearer of bad news but Mr. Stark is in the cemetery at the edge of town."

The panic that had started in her stomach forced its way out of her throat. Gasping, she carefully made her way to a settee in the corner and plopped down.

"There's no use in crying," Thomas said harshly.

Mattie cast him a withering look. "Mr. Langley, I am not crying and if I intended to do so I assure you I would not give you the satisfaction of seeing it." Her coldness turned to suspicion. "And who are you anyway? Why did you meet me at the train? Are you a relative of Mr. Stark's?"

"I'm no kin to Johnny but I guess I was as close to him as anyone around these parts. He owned the ranch next to mine. About a month ago, I came to town to get some supplies and the postmaster gave me the letter you'd sent Johnny saying you were leaving New York City and you'd be here by early spring. It must have been sitting at the post office for a while until he figured out what to do with it. Johnny told me last fall he sent for a bride but when no bride came I thought he'd changed his mind about the whole foolheaded plan," Thomas said.

"I received Mr. Stark's first letter in November and wrote him right away that I was coming," Mattie told him.

"The mail around here is awful slow," the young clerk interjected.

"Why didn't you send a telegram telling me not to come?" Mattie demanded.

"I did. Only it was too late. I got a message back from the Prestons that you were already gone. They suggested I try and stop you in Chicago."

"And did you?"

"I'm running a ranch, woman!" Thomas shouted. "Do you think I can just travel to Chicago and spend days searching the train station? I put an ad in the paper." He reached into his pocket, withdrew a crumpled piece of paper and shoved it at her.

She took it from his hands and carefully unfolded it. "Wife not required," she read aloud. "John Stark of Boxwood, Dakota Territory, is dead. Matilda Robinson is advised to return to New York City." Mattie folded the paper slowly and handed it back to him. "Very direct, Mr. Langley. If I had seen the ad I certainly would not have been confused about its meaning."

Thomas looked at the floor for a moment then gestured outside. "I brought your trunk along. I'm sure the hotel isn't as fancy as you're used to but it's clean and Mrs. Millburn is a fair cook. The train running east will be along in a few days. Get on it and return yourself to New York City."

"I am not a pair of gloves from a mail-order catalog. I cannot just be returned," Mattie said furiously. She stared at him squarely in the eyes until Thomas snorted uncomfortably and turned away.

A thin, greying woman chose that moment to trudge through the hotel entrance carrying a screaming infant. She shoved the child unceremoniously into Thomas' hands.

"Mr. Langley," the woman yelled above the baby's cries. "I cannot take care of this child anymore. She hasn't stopped crying since yesterday afternoon and Mr. Petrie hasn't had a wink of sleep. Nor have I, for that matter."

"You said you could handle her, Mrs. Petrie," Thomas roared.

"I have looked after twenty children in my day and this is the most exhausting. A more sour and ill-tempered child I have never met. I will not keep her anymore," Mrs. Petrie repeated.

The baby thrashed in Thomas' arms, kicking and wailing. The child pitched forward suddenly and would have fallen out of Thomas' awkward grasp if Mattie hadn't caught her. Mattie looked down at the little red scrunched up face, hands balled into tight fists.

"When was the last time she ate?" Mattie asked.

"Last night but she threw up most of it. I've tried this morning but I can't get her to take any milk," Mrs. Petrie answered.

"Last night?" Mattie said angrily. "That is absolutely unacceptable. Did you try giving her some gripe water? Did you properly boil the milk before using it? Have you been swaddling her?"

The older woman bristled at Mattie's reprimand. "I suppose you're an expert? How many children do you have, miss?" She sneered. "The fault doesn't lay with me. This child has been screaming like a banshee since birth." Mrs. Petrie turned to Thomas. "Mr. Langley, you may pay me what you owe me and I'll be off."

Thomas raked a hand through his hair. "Please, Mrs. Petrie. Just a little while longer and I'm sure she'll settle down. I'll pay you a little bit more."

"That child is more trouble than she's worth and I have six of my own to tend to." She held out her hand.

Thomas sighed and withdrew the money from his pocket. Mrs. Petrie snatched it out of his hand and gave Mattie a final cold glare as she passed through the doorway.

"A child is not trouble. A child is a blessing," Mattie said. The baby stopped screaming but continued to fret and moan. She sucked on her fingers and stared up at Mattie with large, blue eyes. "She's beautiful. What's her name?"

"Kathleen," Thomas mumbled.

"I'd say she's about six months old but she seems small. Has a doctor examined her?" Mattie asked. She gently stroked Kathleen's soft cheek and sighed. As much as she had daydreamed about her future as a wife, Mattie had equally imagined being a mother. That dream too had been snatched away from her in an instant and she fought back tears. Mattie gave the baby one last wistful look and handed her to Thomas. He backed away.

"She's fussing. You hold her," he said gruffly.

The young clerk spoke up from behind the counter. "Can I take your trunk to a room, miss?"

Mattie mentally counted the last of her money in her reticule. She had enough money for a room for two nights, three if she skipped a few meals. "Thank you. I suppose that is the only thing to do right now. Perhaps you know of a job available here in town?" she asked the clerk hopefully.

"There ain't no jobs here for decent ladies," Thomas answered.

Mattie turned to him. "Mr. Langley, thank you for meeting my train and delivering the news of Mr. Stark's death. He must have been a very good friend. You needn't feel obliged to concern yourself with my welfare any longer." Giving the little girl one last wistful look, Mattie moved to hand her to Thomas.

"I can't take her." He backed away. "I can't look after a baby."

"Mr. Langley, this is your daughter! You have to take care of her" Mattie said, incredulous.

"I had a woman to look after her until you insulted Mrs. Petrie and made her leave," he said.

Mattie exhaled loudly. "Mrs. Petrie had already made up her mind to leave. Besides, she was horrible. A woman that dour and cross has no business tending to children."

"I could have convinced her," Thomas argued. "There is a limited supply of women in this territory and even fewer who are willing to take on the extra work of looking after a baby that ain't theirs."

"Well, now. There's an idea!" the clerk said brightly. Mattie's trunk was half in, half out the door. Mattie and Thomas turned to look at him. "Miss Robinson here needs a job and you need a lady to look after your little girl. Fortune smiled on the two of you today!"

Thomas rubbed the long scar on his jaw and looked at Mattie. He nodded. "Someone has to look after the child until I find a woman to take her in. I suppose you'll do."

"Those are high words of praise indeed," Mattie said icily.

Realizing that he had hurt her, Thomas gestured to the baby. "I meant that she seems to have taken to you."

"I've been looking after children since I was a child myself," Mattie said. "I know how to deal with a crying baby."

"I can't do much more than pay for your room and meals here at the hotel," Thomas told her.

The clerk stumbled hastily past Mattie's trunk. "No. Not here. Not at this hotel. A baby crying and carrying on at all hours of the day? My guests would not like that. I'm sorry."

Thomas threw his hands up. "I guess you'll have to stay at my house with the child. It's not permanent. It's just until I find a place for her."

Mattie smiled and a dimple appeared in one cheek, catching Thomas off guard. He was surprised at how much he liked seeing a woman smile. "And while you're looking for a permanent place for Kathleen, I'll secure a position here in town or to come up with another plan." Suddenly Mattie's smile faded. "Is it appropriate? Two unmarried people in the same house without a chaperone?"

She was right, Thomas thought. Even out here there were some rules of respectability that shouldn't be broken. "I'll stay in Johnny's lean-to. You stay in my house with the child."

Mattie nodded her head. "That seems an appropriate arrangement, Mr. Langley."

"I have work to do. We'd best be going. The wagon's outside the general store." Stooping to grab her trunk, Thomas hoisted it upon one shoulder and stomped toward the general store. Mattie gave a quick wave to the clerk and followed. Her long legs didn't have any trouble keeping pace with his and soon she found herself standing in front of a wagon attached to two bay horses.

"I hate to trouble you, Mr. Langley," Mattie started.

"I'm not sure that you do, Miss Robinson," Thomas retorted.

"I just want to make sure you have everything I'll be needing for Kathleen at your house," she said. Thomas stared at her, a blank look on his face. "Blankets, diapers, clothing," Mattie suggested.

"She went right to Mrs. Petrie's house after she was born. Mrs. Petrie must have provided for her. I don't have anything." Thomas looked away, unable to meet her eyes.

"Perhaps you could make a few small purchases at the store?" Mattie suggested gently.

Thomas nodded and loaded her trunk into the wagon. Together they walked up the wide plank stairs and into the store.

A bell on the door jingled happily as they entered. An older woman, her silver hair braided into an intricate bun at the back of her head, looked up from the counter and smiled when she saw Mattie. When her gaze fell onto Thomas she gave a stiff nod in his direction.

"Good morning, miss," she said.

"Good morning," Mattie replied. "I need to pick up some things for this little girl."

The clerk peered into the bundle of blankets in Mattie's arms. "The poor dear. She looks very unhappy."

"I'm sure she's hungry," Mattie said.

The clerk leaned toward Mattie and spoke quietly. "I'm Mrs. Telford and this is my store. There's a small private parlor just through those doors. Please, go in and feed your baby."

Mattie blushed. "That's very kind, Mrs. Telford but this isn't my child. This is Mr. Langley's daughter." She looked toward Thomas.

"Mr. Langley? Surely to goodness you're not..." Mrs. Telford stopped and pinched her lips together. "Well, come along, dear and we'll get everything together."

Thomas lounged against a display case, hat in hand. Like almost everyone in Boxwood, Mrs. Telford eyed him with suspicion and kept her distance. It didn't bother him; he liked it better that way. He just wanted to be left alone and in peace to live out what remained of his life.

He shook his head as he watched Mrs. Telford show Mattie bolts of fabric. They would be here all day at this rate, jawing and fretting over which pattern or color to buy. Thomas tapped his boot impatiently. Several minutes passed before Mattie decided and Mrs. Telford took the chosen bolt of fabric to the back to be cut and wrapped. The bell on the door jingled and a short, stocky man ambled in. Thomas resisted the urge to spit. Eli Watson was a miserable excuse for a man. How many times had he seen Eli's late wife with a black eye and a busted up lip? How many times had he seen his children, thin and dirty, sitting outside the saloon in the shantytown waiting for him?

Seeing Mattie, Eli let out a low whistle. "Johnny Stark sure did well for hisself. Too bad he ain't around to see it." The man laughed loudly.

"I beg your pardon?" Mattie asked. Thomas expected her to shrink back in shock at the man's rough manners but instead, Mattie stared him down, a look of derision on her face.

"You're not much to look at but you're nice and sturdy," the man continued, looking her up and down. "Looks like you're a good worker. I don't even mind that you come with a baby. Makes no nevermind to me. I've got eight at home and no woman. Since Johnny's dead, I'll marry you. I'll keep you fed and make sure you've got a nice warm place to sleep at night," he winked.

"Move on, Eli," Thomas said in a low rumble. He stood up to his full height and walked slowly across the store. The few customers in the store stopped talking and all eyes turned to Thomas.

"I was having a private conversation with the lady. Asking her if she wants to be my bride, in fact. What business is it of yours?" Eli asked.

"She's mine," Thomas said through clenched teeth. "Move on."

Eli stared at Thomas for a few seconds then put his hands up. "Alright. I didn't know. I don't want no trouble." He turned and scurried out of the store.

Thomas shoved his hat on his head. "I'll wait in the wagon. Hurry up," he told Mattie.

CHAPTER THREE

S he's mine.

Those words echoed in Thomas' head long after he helped Mattie and the baby into the wagon and set off for home. He misspoke. It wasn't what he meant. He just couldn't stand the way Eli Watson looked Mattie up and down. It wasn't...polite. He spoke without thinking, is all. It sounded like he was making a claim on her but it wasn't like that. He just needed someone to look after his daughter. Thomas cursed silently. By sundown Mrs. Telford and her quilting group, two of whom were in the store at the time, would have spread that juicy piece of gossip all over town.

Thomas cast a furtive glance at the woman sitting beside him. She was striking, with smooth skin, thick brown hair and a smattering of freckles across the bridge of her nose.

She was tall with a commanding presence but he marveled at how gracefully she moved. She was also blessed with a preponderance of curves that even her matronly beige traveling suit couldn't hide. He looked away quickly, disgusted with himself. He had no business thinking about a woman in that way.

The wagon lurched along the trail out of town and Mattie's turned and shifted in her seat, her head swiveling from one direction to the other, trying to take in every detail of the immense prairie. She reached out a hand and let the long grasses run through her fingers.

"Don't do that," Thomas barked. "You'll fall out of the wagon and be crushed under the wheels."

Mattie withdrew her hand quickly. "I hadn't thought of that. You're right. I should be more careful, especially when I'm holding a child."

Thomas swallowed and looked away uncomfortably. His mother would have tanned his hide if she'd heard him speak so harshly to a woman.

They passed a few minutes in silence until Mattie said, "It's so quiet here."

Thomas snorted. She hadn't even been here for a day and already the complaining had begun.

Mattie looked down and smoothed the baby's forehead. Kathleen had been lulled to sleep by the motion of the moving wagon but continued to move and whimper while she slept. "Have you lived in Boxwood long, Mr. Langley?" she asked.

"A while," he said.

"I've never lived anywhere but New York City," Mattie told him.

"Well, this ain't New York City," Thomas told her.

"I should hope not. The noise and dirt and people pushing and rushing about, as if everyone is doing something of utmost importance all the time. I can imagine out here you could actually hear yourself think," she said.

Thomas grunted. The last thing he wanted to do was hear his own thoughts. He worked hard and kept himself busy so he didn't have time to think. If he started thinking he'd start remembering.

"I assume your wife passed in childbirth?" Mattie asked gently. Thomas gave her a curt nod. "I am very sorry for both you and Kathleen. It happens far too often, I'm afraid."

Thomas choked down the lump that was building in his throat. "You know something about that?"

"My own mother succumbed a few hours after I was born. I was raised by Dr. and Mrs. Preston. Dr. Preston has a small practice on the east side of New York City. Have you ever been to New York, Mr. Langley?" Without waiting for him to reply she continued on. "The east side is quite possibly the poorest, dirtiest, most dangerous areas of the city. Doc is a blessing to the neighborhood. In my twenty-six years I saw my fair share of women pass away after having their babies. It didn't get any easier; it just made me angrier and more determined to find a better situation for myself. Which is why I answered Mr. Stark's request for a wife. You probably wonder what kind of a woman would agree to marry a man she'd never met before."

Thomas shook his head. "Ain't none of my business."

"No, I suppose it's not," Mattie said. "I want you to be confident that I know what I'm doing, Mr. Langley. I've been helping with babies and children ever since I can remember and when I was old enough I started helping Doc with births. He said I had a real gift for it. I was supposed to go into service when I was fourteen and I did for a short time but there was...an incident. Several incidents, actually."

Thomas raised an eyebrow.

A worried look spread over Mattie's face. "I suppose I should be forthcoming since you are employing me. The first time I was sent to the home of Dr. and Mrs. Bradley but was dismissed after a week. Mrs. Bradley said my incessant talking gave her a headache. If you ask me it wasn't my incessant talking but her incessant drinking that gave her a headache. Then I was sent to be a companion to Mrs. Abbott who was a very dear and sweet elderly woman. My talking didn't seem to bother her. Unfortunately, while making her afternoon tea I started a small fire in the kitchen. Nobody was hurt, thank goodness, but her son fired me. My last employment was with Mr. and Mrs. Appleby. Mrs. Appleby was strict but fair but Mr. Appleby was a scoundrel. One evening he followed me into the kitchen and.." she glanced at Thomas, "attempted to take liberties with me. I hit him over the head with a frying pan."

Thomas let out a loud snort. He was so surprised at the sound that for a few seconds he looked around trying to find its source until he realized with a shock that the sound had come from him. How long had it been since he'd laughed? How long had it been since he'd been truly delighted by something? It had been years, he realized. Since before the war.

"Oh, Mr. Langley. It wasn't funny at all. Thankfully the cad wasn't hurt or I could have been in terrible trouble. I thought for sure that the Applebys would call for a policeman and I'd be off to prison for assaulting a gentleman but Mrs. Appleby told Mr. Gardner to bring out some ice for Mr. Appleby's head and told Cook to send Mr. Appleby's dinner to his room. She sent me to my room and fired me the next morning, though she was awfully kind about it. I didn't seem capable of doing much more than helping Dr. Preston with his patients. My options were very limited, Mr. Langley, which led me to Boxwood and to Mr. Stark."

You'll find your options are even more limited out here, thought Thomas smugly. There are no cooks or servants or policemen out here. The first time you hear coyotes howling steps from your door or you have to take shelter from your first raging lightning storm you'll be begging me to put you on the next train east.

They continued in silence until the wagon reached the top of a small slope that looked down on Thomas' house. Mattie gasped. "Is that your farm?"

Thomas held back his anger. The ranch may not be much by her standards but it was everything to him. "Out here we call it a ranch and we've been on my land since we left the main road," Thomas told her.

"It's beautiful," Mattie whispered in awe. "The house... it's so...it looks like it belongs in a dream."

Thomas glanced at her, confused by her reaction. The small house and simple barn didn't compare to the fine houses she must have seen in New York City. The barn was just large enough to hold a few cows, his three horses, a goat, a sow and her piglets. He kept a dozen chickens in their coop next to the barnyard where they'd be safe from hungry predators at night. The little, whitewashed house only had three rooms downstairs and a loft above the parlor but it held the wicked Dakota snow and wind at bay. It was the front porch that was truly magnificent and had taken him the longest to build. It ran the entire length of the house along the ground floor and along the upper loft. He had spent hours carving each spindle of the railing and each piece of gingerbread trim, trying as best he could to replicate the porch at Belle Haven, Susannah's childhood home. He had hoped it would bring his wife joy but it only increased her longing for South Carolina.

Thomas stopped the wagon at the front door and jumped out to hold the horses, forcing Mattie to lay Kathleen on the floor of the wagon and climb down. The baby was awake and beginning to fret. She reached out a tiny hand and grasped Mattie's finger. Wrapping her tightly in a new blanket, Mattie walked up to the front door of the little house, stopping on the porch. She touched a piece of the trim gently with a long delicate finger. "Did you carve this?" she asked. Thomas nodded. Mattie gazed at the porch in wonder. "It's truly beautiful, Mr. Langley. Kathleen is a very lucky child to grow up here."

Gruffly, Thomas pushed past her and opened the door. The house smelled closed up and stale. He looked around at the kitchen, noticing for the first time the thick layer of dust that had settled on everything except the table and his chair. The breakfast dishes sat unwashed on the table next to a lopsided loaf of bread he had attempted to make the day before. The frying pan on top of the cookstove was full of hardened grease and some leftover potatoes. He quickly opened up a small window near the stove. How had the state of the kitchen eluded him, he wondered. Why hadn't he noticed before now?

Kathleen let out a loud cry. Mattie held her upright and rubbed her back. "This little girl isn't going to wait any longer for her dinner," Mattie told him. "Bread soaked in water will have to do for now but I'll need to prepare some milk for her to drink later."

Thomas grabbed the milk pail near the washbasin. "Bread's there," he gestured to the table. "The water in the basin's clean."

As Thomas opened the door to leave, a cinnamon colored dog with white paws ran into the kitchen, barking and wagging its tail in greeting. He stopped in front of Mattie and sniffed.

"Aren't you beautiful!" Mattie leaned down to pet him on the head. "What's his name?"

Thomas snorted. "He's a dog. Call him Dog." He stomped across the floor with the milk pail and disappeared outside.

Mattie watched the dog stretch out near the stove and rest his head on his paws. "I'm not calling you Dog," she told him. "That's ridiculous. Dogs are supposed to have names, just like people." The dog cocked his head quizzically at her and perked up his ears. She looked at his white front paws. "What about Socks? I know it's not a very manly name but I think it suits you." She bent down and scratched Socks behind the ear. He whined happily and licked her hand.

With Kathleen on her hip, Mattie cut a piece of bread from the loaf and put it into a small bowl. She poured fresh water from the basin into the bowl and waited until the bread soaked up enough water to become a soft mash. Kathleen's little body trembled as her cries turned to screams and her hands clenched into tiny fists. Sitting down at the table, Mattie put a small amount of the mash into Kathleen's mouth. The baby took it and sucked away greedily. Kathleen finished a whole slice of bread by the time Thomas returned.

"Thank you, Mr. Langley. Should I prepare supper tonight?" Mattie asked as Thomas stomped across the floor and deposited the milk pail on the table.

"Don't worry about me. Look after the child," he grunted. Thomas turned around and went back out the door, slamming it shut behind him.

Mattie sniffled and cuddled Kathleen close. Up until this morning she'd been so full of hope and excitement. Now it all seemed to be draining away, leaving her feeling empty and alone, uncertain of her future. She wiped away a tear stubbornly. Mrs. Preston always told her to put away her tears and soldier on, she reminded herself. She used to say that things have a habit of working themselves out, though Mattie couldn't imagine how this mess would work itself out. She let out a deep sigh and held Kathleen closer. The baby burrowed into Mattie's chest and looked up at her with heavy eyes.

Mattie looked around the kitchen for anything she could use as a cradle. Finding nothing, she hesitantly peeked through a doorway at the far end of the kitchen and looked into a parlor. It was a simple but comfortable room, bare except for a settee and a wooden rocking chair beside the fireplace. The walls held only two small tintypes in matching frames. Mattie looked at them closely. The first was of a large white house with a wide porch and verandah along the second story. She had seen enough houses just like that in newspapers during the war to know that the picture must have been taken somewhere in the South. The second frame held a picture of Thomas and a petite light-haired woman. The woman sat in a high backed chair, her hands placed gracefully in her lap and her head held high. Thomas stood beside her clutching the top of the chair. Neither smiled.

A worn quilt was rolled up in a messy ball at the end of the settee. "It may not be a cradle," she told Kathleen. "But I'll fold it into a pad and you can lay down for a while." Mattie picked up the quilt with one hand and shook it. A man's shirt fell onto the floor. Thomas had been sleeping on the settee she realized, holding up the shirt. She couldn't imagine such a large man being able to sleep comfortably on the short and narrow piece of furniture. Why was he disrobing and sleeping in the parlor? Mattie blushed. She shouldn't be thinking of Mr. Langley sleeping anywhere and she certainly shouldn't be thinking of him disrobing.

While Kathleen napped restlessly, Mattie prepared some milk for her dinner. She brought the milk slowly to a boil on the stove and added molasses until it turned into a thick light brown syrup. She let the milk cool in jars placed inside a pan of cold water.

Thomas had purchased diaper cloth at the general store and Mattie set about ripping it into smaller squares that she could fold into diapers. When she finished, Mattie surveyed her work stacked in three neat little piles on the kitchen table then groaned. She needed straight pins to secure the sides of the diaper and she hadn't asked Thomas to purchase some. It was possible to tie the sides but from her experience, Mattie knew that she'd spend most of her time tying and re-tying the sides of the diaper. *A sewing box! Mattie thought. There must be a sewing box somewhere with pins. And if I found some thread and a needle I could finish the edges of the diapers so they wouldn't continue to fray.*

Mattie looked through the parlor and opened every cupboard in the kitchen but found nothing. Just outside the door to the parlor she hesitantly peered up a set of stairs to the second floor loft. She was sure Thomas wouldn't want her searching through his personal belongings. Still, she reasoned, without pins the diapers were useless and Thomas had hired her to look after his baby, hadn't he? Mattie grasped the railing and climbed the narrow stairs to the second floor.

Two large windows let in enough light for Mattie to see that the upper level only contained a large bed frame without a mattress and a plain wooden armoire. A thin layer of dust coated the floorboards and even though the bright afternoon sun shone through the windows the room seemed cold and forlorn.

Mattie crossed the room and opened the armoire. Half a dozen dresses hung on pegs, clean and neatly pressed. She touched the delicate lace collar on a pretty light blue calico dress. A dark green day dress caught her eye and Mattie pulled it out to examine the precise and even stitches on the fitted bodice. Holding it up, her mouth gaped at the size of the dress. Thomas' wife couldn't have been five feet tall and judging from the dress' tiny waist and narrow shoulders she hadn't weighed very much either. Mattie had always felt like a giant oaf, awkward and clumsy next to girls like that.

Looking down, some light colored material piled on the floor caught her eye. She bent down to examine it more closely and discovered two piles of diapers and several knitted diaper covers. Rectangular layers of plain white cotton flannel had been sewn together, some with red thread and some with blue, to make diapers. Beside the pile of diapers, Mattie found a tin box of straight pins and a doll made of flannel and cotton rags. She picked up the doll and turned it over in her hands. She inhaled deeply to keep from crying. Mattie's heart ached for the woman who had so lovingly made these for her baby but never had the chance to use them. She suddenly felt like an intruder, as if she was snooping through a woman's journal that held all of her private hopes and dreams. Mattie quickly gathered up the diapers, pins and the doll and hurried back downstairs.

Alone that afternoon, Mattie took the opportunity to study Kathleen closely. Despite being very small and underweight she seemed to be progressing as expected for a child of her age. She followed Mattie's finger with her eyes and reached out to grasp it. When Mattie rolled her on her stomach Kathleen kicked her legs and held up her head briefly by herself. They spent the better part of an hour nose to nose while Mattie sang her songs and Kathleen touched Mattie's face. Sadly, Mattie suspected that Kathleen hadn't been given much attention or stimulation from Mrs. Petrie.

Occasionally Mattie heard Thomas call to the horses in the field but saw nothing of him until dinnertime when he stalked across the yard and disappeared into the barn. The only other indication that he hadn't completely abandoned her in the middle of the desolate prairie was a faint light shining across the field that night from what Mattie could only guess was Mr. Stark's cabin.

CHAPTER FOUR

*H*e shivered uncontrollably in the savage cold. He tried to pull his knees up to his chest for warmth but his body was immovable. Dampness seeped in through the torn paper and cloth he'd used to plug the holes in his boots. Groans of pain and hunger rang out all around him. Water. He needed water. He crawled on his belly, hands grasping at the frozen ground, until he reached a puddle that had formed in a depression in the mud made by a large bootprint. Reaching out a hand, he clawed its surface and broke through the thin skim of ice. He drank from the puddle like a dog, lapping greedily. When he could take no more of the putrid water, he lifted his head slowly and allowed his eyes to focus. Inches from his face a hand grasped a small wooden cross with waxy blue fingers. His gaze traveled up the hand to the arm and then to the face. The cheekbones stuck out sharply against the sunken cheeks, *lips contorted in a grimace that showed a row of rotten teeth. The mouth hung wide open, as if the soldier had died screaming. The eyes looked at him in horror.*

Thomas awoke with a start in the darkness, his heart pounding in his chest and gasping for air. He gripped the arms of Old Johnny's rocking chair and concentrated on getting his loud, ragged breathing under control. Jerking and unsteady, he stood and pulled the sweat soaked shirt from his body and threw it onto the steel outline of the bed frame. Thomas rubbed his stiff neck and bent sideways to try and stretch out his back. His left side ached from his knee to his shoulder. He knew from experience that he would not go back to sleep.

Thomas waited until sunrise before he left the cabin and walked across the field to his house. He was in the barnyard when he heard the loud screams of an unhappy baby. Making his way to the house, he opened the front door cautiously and entered the kitchen.

Mattie greeted him with a tired smile. She had dark circles under her eyes and several strands of her hair had escaped its plait. She was still wearing her traveling suit from the day before which was now wrinkled and dirty. Mattie paced up and down the length of the room, rocking Kathleen in her arms as the baby wailed. Wet towels hung on the backs of chairs and a scrub brush and a pail of water sat in one corner. A mound of dirty diapers filled a wash bucket near the door.

"I've fed her three times since suppertime yesterday and she hasn't managed to keep any of it down," Mattie said above the cries.

Thomas hadn't been in the kitchen a minute and already the screaming was grating on him. He couldn't imagine listening to the child cry for hours upon hours. "She's been like this since birth. No one knows what's wrong with her."

"I've had plenty of time to think it over, Mr. Langley. I suppose some of Kathleen's crying could be caused by colic but I've never seen colic that looks like this and I've seen my share of colicky babies. Colic usually has a pattern, starting and stopping around the same time every day. Kathleen seems to just cry all the time. And this little girl is hungry! She wants to eat but every time she does it comes right back up," Mattie told him. "That got me thinking. Yesterday afternoon I fed Kathleen bread soaked in water and she was fine. Then last night I fed her boiled milk and molasses and she's been sick ever since. I think it's possible that Kathleen can't stomach cow's milk. It's very rare; I've only seen it once before, but sometimes cow's milk makes a baby sick. I suppose you have a goat?"

Thomas gave a curt nod.

"I'll try feeding her some bread soaked in goat's milk with molasses and see if that helps," Mattie said.

Wordlessly, Thomas grabbed the milk bucket. Feelings of guilt enveloped him. A good father wouldn't delight in escaping his crying child. A good father would take care of his daughter instead of sending her to live with strangers. He would know how to calm and soothe her. A good father would hold his daughter in his arms. *I've never been a good father, just like I was never a good husband*, Thomas thought bitterly.

When he returned fifteen minutes later with the pail full of goat's milk, Kathleen's cries had turned into short, piercing screams.

With gentle hands Mattie unwrapped the blankets and pulled up the baby's long muslin gown. "Her belly's hard," she told Thomas. "All that crying has caused her to swallow air. It's giving her painful cramps."

Thomas placed the pail of goat's milk on the table without looking at Kathleen or Mattie and turned to leave. Mattie grabbed his arm. He jerked it back as if he'd been burned.

Mattie's withdrew her hand slowly. "I have to get her food ready. I need you to help her get rid of the air that's built up in her belly." Mattie put Kathleen down on the blanket near the stove. The baby screamed louder.

"I can't do it," Thomas backed away and put up his hands protectively. "I don't know anything about babies!"

Mattie stared at him sharply. "For goodness sake, Mr. Langley! Your daughter is suffering and she needs you. You can do it and you will do it."

Thomas knew from her determined tone and the set of her mouth that Mattie wouldn't allow him to walk away. He knelt slowly on the floor.

"Take one leg at a time, bend it gently and bring it up to her chest," Mattie instructed.

Thomas reached forward then dropped his hands and shook his head. "I can't do it. Her legs are too small." He paused then said quietly. "I'm afraid I'll break them."

Mattie laughed then smiled at him kindly. "She is not a doll made of porcelain, Mr. Langley. Your daughter is stronger than you think. She's lived this long, hasn't she?"

Awkwardly, he picked up one of Kathleen's legs. He hadn't been able to help his wife but he could at least try to help his daughter.

With the baby fed and sleeping in the parlor, Mattie wished desperately to lie down too but the neglected kitchen needed a thorough cleaning. The soiled diapers, towels, and clothing needed to be soaked in hot water before they could be washed with soap. Several times throughout the night Kathleen brought up the entire contents of her stomach and the kitchen floor was marked with streaks where Mattie tried to clean up quickly. She propped the door open to let in some fresh air while she filled pail after pail of water from the pump in the yard and scrubbed every surface of the kitchen. She set the laundry tub on the porch and filled it with water and dirty linens. She had just changed into a fresh dress and was preparing to sit down for a cup of tea when she noticed a dot moving across the horizon. As it came closer to the ranch she could see it was a buckboard pulled by two white horses.

She glanced about. Thomas was in the back pasture with his herd of cattle. He wouldn't hear her if she yelled for him. She whistled and Socks came bounding out of the barn where he'd taken shelter from the midday sun. He sat down at her feet on the porch. Perhaps she should go inside and lock the door. She'd heard the territory could be dangerous, full of outlaws and violent men.

What foolishness! Mattie scolded herself. *A dangerous outlaw is hardly going to come riding up in a buckboard.* She squinted and looked more closely as the visitor approached the house. *And dangerous outlaws certainly don't wear three-piece suits.* It was more likely that he was a salesman of some kind or a preacher who'd ventured from the main road and lost his way.

The man guided the horses down the lane and stopped in front of her. He was a stout older man, his short white hair oiled flat and his Van Dyke expertly trimmed. He descended from the buckboard and used his hat to shake the dust from his crisp brown linen suit. He looked her up and down with a condescending smile causing Mattie to take an instant dislike to him.

"You speak English?" he bellowed, a strong Southern lilt to his voice.

"I do indeed, sir," Mattie answered coldly.

"Well, I can never be sure around these parts. It's full of Indians and immigrants," he spat. "Who are you?"

"Who are you?" Mattie countered.

"Augustus Hendricks," the man answered. He doffed his hat to her.

"Well, Mr. Hendricks, we are in need of nothing you are selling. Good day," she said dismissively and turned to go back into the house.

"I'm here to see Tom Langley. Why don't you go fetch your man?" Hendricks asked with a wink.

Mattie's blood boiled at his familiar gesture. "Mr. Langley is not my man."

Hendricks snickered. "An unfortunate turn of phrase. I meant no disrespect," he said, dismissively. "I had no idea Tom found himself a wife. May I extend to you my best wishes on your marriage? "

"I am Miss Robinson. I am employed to care for Mr. Langley's child." Mattie told him.

"Well, Miss Robinson it is a pleasure to meet you. Be a dear and go and fetch your employer for me," Hendricks said.

Mattie stared at him, her expression icy. "I'm not a dog, Mr. Hendricks. I don't fetch."

"Hendricks!" a deep, gruff voice shouted. Mattie looked

up to see Thomas walking through the barnyard.

"Oh, Tom, there you are. I was just talking to your lovely employee. She neglected to invite me in for a cool drink on this hot day but isn't that just like a Yankee? They're not known for their hospitality, are they?" Mr. Hendricks said.

Thomas approached the porch with long strides. Mattie could tell from his face that Thomas didn't care for Hendricks any more than she did. "What do you want, Hendricks?" Thomas growled.

"I came to discuss business with you," he answered. "More specifically, I came to remind you that you have a loan that needs repaying."

"You'll get your money at the end of the season when I sell off some of my cattle, just like it says in our agreement," Thomas said.

"So you've said. But I keep hearing that cattle prices are dropping and there's all that trouble with the railroad and the Indians. What if you can't get those cattle to market? What if you get those cattle to market but they're worthless? So many terrible thoughts keep me awake at night. If you can't pay me come fall then I'd have no choice but to call in my loan and you'd lose this farm. And I would feel terrible about that, Tom, really I would."

"You'll get your money," Thomas repeated.

"I know. So you've said. But in order to save myself some sleepless nights I've come here in good faith today to offer you a way out. You sell this property to me for a slightly discounted price and I'll forgive your loan. This backward, uncivilized territory has enough land open for homesteading. It won't take you long to find another home for you and your..." Hendricks paused. "Nanny."

"Get off my land," Thomas said, his voice a deep growl.

"Tom, I'm offering you a great deal. You need to think about it," Hendricks urged.

"Get off my land now or I'll put you off my land," Thomas told him.

Mr. Hendricks' smiled faded. "You better hope you can sell those cattle, Langley, because when September rolls around I'm coming for my money."

Thomas stared at him, arms crossed and continued staring long after Hendricks climbed back onto the buckboard and headed down the lane toward the main road.

"What a horrible man," Mattie said. "Telling me to fetch you like I was a dog! The nerve! And the way he kept calling me your nanny and your employee, insinuating I was your whore."

Thomas turned at her use of language and stared, wide-eyed.

Mattie waved a hand. "Oh please, Mr. Langley. I haven't exactly lived a sheltered life. Our neighborhood was full of brothels and I've been in every single one of them to stitch up or bandage or tend to the poor women who work there. I've helped deliver a good many children in those places too."

Mattie paused. "You don't really think he'd take your land if you weren't able to pay him all the money you owe him, do you? Surely if you had most of it he'd give you more time."

"I wouldn't count on it. He put a whole family off their ranch last year when they came up short with their loan payment," Thomas told her.

Mattie furrowed her brow. "Augustus Hendricks," she said.

"That's him." He looked at Mattie. "What?"

She shook her head. "It's funny but I feel like I've heard that name before. It sounds so familiar."

Thomas shrugged. "It's a common enough name, I guess. Must be hundreds of Hendricks in New York City, maybe even thousands."

"You're probably right," Mattie conceded.

Thomas took off his hat and ran an arm along his forehead. "The next time someone comes up to the house, get inside and lock the door. A woman alone out here is a target. Lots of unpleasant things can happen."

"As I told you before, Mr. Langley, I am well aware of the unpleasant things that can happen to both men and women. I didn't grow up on Fifth Avenue."

"Stay inside with the door locked," Thomas repeated. He set his hat back on his head and stalked back to the barnyard.

Mattie turned to Socks. "Nor am I used to being ordered about by a cantankerous man," she told the dog. Even if she did find his eyes strangely captivating.

Mattie surveyed the small garden. She could just barely make out some carrots and green beans, several rows of corn and a large section that looked like it could be potatoes. Weeds grew everywhere, obscuring the straight rows she was sure Thomas had planted. She stooped down and examined some cabbages that had been gnawed on by rabbits.

"What are we going to do about this?" Mattie asked Kathleen.

Kathleen sucked her fingers and patted Mattie's face. Kathleen had only slept for two hours but she awoke happy and had kept down the goat's milk and bread. Mattie placed Kathleen on the grass and picked up a hoe to get to work. Immediately the infant started sobbing.

"I see," said Mattie, dropping the hoe and picking up Kathleen. "You're a needy child but I can't blame you for that. You haven't had the proper attention your mama would have given you." Mattie hoped that Thomas would find someone to look after Kathleen who would hold her and play with her, show her some attention and love. Children needed so much more than food and shelter to thrive. Mattie knew this first hand. If Doctor and Mrs. Preston hadn't shown her the love and kindness they did,

Mattie shuddered to think where she might be now. There were so many abandoned women and girls who turned to lives of crime and became victims of violence.

Mattie tickled Kathleen's feet and the baby gurgled happily. It seemed that she would have to work on the garden while carrying a baby. Thinking about a solution, she remembered Mrs. Murphy and some of the other ladies who used to carry their babies in a sling around their neck and shoulders while they collected laundry for washing. Mattie ran quickly to the parlor to retrieve the sheet from the settee. She folded it into a triangle, tied two ends together and slung it across one shoulder and under the opposite arm. Mattie carefully placed Kathleen in the folds of the fabric. The child peeked out every now and then to gaze up at Mattie's face but seemed content to simply feel the warmth of Mattie's body.

She finished hoeing two rows of carrots and was starting on the beans when she heard Socks bark loudly from the front step. She walked around to the front of the house and saw a wagon approaching. She threw down the hoe, annoyed that Hendricks had returned but when she looked carefully she could see the driver was a woman. Had Thomas found someone to look after Kathleen already? Automatically, Mattie's hand reached for Kathleen and held onto her tiny little hand gently.

The wagon stopped in the barnyard and the driver waved. The young woman's long blonde curls fell to her waist and she wore a simple day dress. As she slid carefully from the wagon, the slight roundness of her belly revealed that she was expecting a child. She walked over to Mattie, her smile friendly.

"I apologize for coming to call so soon after you've just arrived and are getting settled but I just had to come by and introduce myself. I'm Alice Taylor," she said. "My husband Will and I live on the next ranch over."

"I'm very pleased to meet you. I'm Mattie Robinson," She smoothed her hair and brushed some dirt from her dress. "I apologize for my appearance. I must look a mess."

"Don't give it a second thought. I can see I've caught you in the middle of a very large job," Alice gestured to the garden.

Kathleen peeped out of the sling sucking her thumb, her blues eyes wide and curious.

Alice gasped. "I didn't know there was a baby in there."

Mattie laughed. "She cries if I put her down so at least with this I can get some work done."

"What a clever thing!" Alice said, examining the sling. "I'll have to do the same when this little one comes." She rubbed her belly gently.

"You must be about four months along?" Mattie asked.

"How did you know?" Alice answered.

"I've taken care of children and expectant mothers most of my life," Mattie told her.

Alice's eyes lit up. "Really? That's wonderful. There isn't a doctor in these parts and my mother is in Fort Laramie. I write to her, of course, but sometimes I have questions and Will is, well, Will is…"

"Shy about those matters?" Mattie finished.

Alice laughed. "I was going to say uncomfortable. When I talk about the baby he starts babbling and telling me how different farm animals give birth and rear their young."

Mattie gestured to the front porch. "Would you like to sit down? I can bring some chairs out on the porch. I'm afraid I don't have much to offer you except water and some biscuits I made this morning."

"That would be lovely!" Alice said.

Both women installed themselves on the porch. Socks lay protectively at Mattie's feet.

"I wanted to come by and make sure you were alright." Alice took a bite of her biscuit, followed by a large drink of water.

"How kind of you," Mattie said. "I admit I was shocked and saddened, of course, that Mr. Stark had passed away. I was very much looking forward to meeting him and marrying him."

"Actually, I wanted to make sure you were faring well here with Mr. Langley," Alice clarified. "Mr. Langley is a rather unpleasant man."

Mattie nodded her head. "That he is. But I suspect he is a good man who has endured a great deal of anguish. Was he always this way?"

Alice nodded. "Will and I tried several times to be neighborly but Mr. Langley told us very clearly to leave him alone. I stopped by right after Susannah passed away to express my condolences and he grumbled a thank you and shut the door on my face."

"Susannah was his wife?" Mattie asked.

Alice nodded. "Poor Susannah. She was such a sad woman and always ill, even before the baby." Alice leaned in closer to Mattie. "I could tell that she was real homesick for South Carolina. It was strange. On one hand she seemed very lonely but on the other she didn't want people to come calling or to attend any of Boxwood's social events." Alice sighed and brought a hand to her mouth. "You must think that I'm a terrible gossip and a horrible woman to speak ill of the dead."

"Not at all," Mattie reassured her. "You haven't said anything unkind."

Mattie pulled Kathleen onto her lap and hugged her.

"You're so good with her," Alice said. "Maybe Mr. Langley will keep you on as his nanny and housekeeper."

Mattie shook her head. "He keeps reminding me that this arrangement is only temporary. He's looking for another woman to take in Kathleen."

"There isn't a woman in Boxwood who would be willing to take that child. Mrs. Petrie has recounted in great detail how horrible she was to live with, what with the constant crying and spitting up. Plus, I daresay there isn't anyone in town who wants to deal with Mr. Langley."

Kathleen let out a whimper and buried her head in Mattie's chest.

"It looks like this little girl is hungry again. That's a very good sign." Mattie said.

"I must get back home. I told Will I wouldn't be very long and he worries constantly about me. He made me promise I wouldn't take the horses any faster than a slow walk and that I wouldn't jump down from the wagon. And he made me promise about a million other things that I've since forgotten." Alice set down her half-finished biscuit and a glass of water. "I also would like to invite you to Boxwood's annual spring picnic. Winter here is brutal and keeps us pretty much confined to our homes. Once spring comes and the roads become passable again it's a cause for celebration."

"That sounds wonderful," Mattie said, genuinely touched that Alice had thought of her.

"Bring a dish to share for the noon meal and the ground is still pretty wet so I suggest some blankets too. We all get together in the field behind the general store. Do you think Mr. Langley will bring you into town?"

"I hadn't thought of that," Mattie said.

"I did," Alice said proudly. "Will and I will drive by on Sunday and if you need a ride, just hang a blanket from the clothesline. We'll be able to see it from the ridge."

"Thank you! That's so kind of you. Perhaps I can make some inquiries at the picnic to see if anyone is looking for a nanny or any general household help, even if it's just for room and board right now."

Alice smiled slyly. "More than a few young men noticed you getting off the train. And I happen to know that some were downright overjoyed when they learned you wouldn't be getting married. You could be married by this time next week if you wanted to."

"Don't be silly," Mattie said. "If any men noticed me it was because I take up the space usually reserved for two women."

"Now who's being silly? You are an elegant woman, Miss Robinson. Who wouldn't want to marry you?" Alice said.

"Mr. Langley, for one," Mattie blurted out. She could feel her face redden with a burst of heat.

"How interesting," Alice smirked.

"Not that I wish to marry Mr. Langley, of course," Mattie said quickly. "He's horribly rude and a terrible conversationalist."

Alice looked up at the midday sky. "I must get going before Will sends out a search party for me. You will come on Sunday, won't you?" Alice asked.

"Absolutely! I am looking forward to it," Mattie assured her.

Mattie couldn't for the life of her figure out how she was going to persuade a man who wanted nothing to do with people to attend Boxwood's first social event of the spring, especially a man as stubborn as Thomas Langley.

CHAPTER FIVE

Thomas paused, his hand on the doorknob of the front door, wondering if he should knock. *Have I become completely addled? This is my house!* he thought angrily. Mattie Robinson hadn't been in Boxwood two days and she'd already become an irritation. She interrupted his work, took over his house and refused to listen to him. No, the sooner she was gone the better. Bringing her and the child to the farm had been a mistake. Neither of them belonged here. He'd done right by Johnny, meeting Mattie at the train station and explaining everything but now she needed to be on her way; where she went and with who wasn't his business. And he couldn't look after a baby and work a farm. He didn't know the first thing about looking after a child, let alone a girl. Besides, his daughter deserved better than to be raised by the likes of him. Tomorrow he would go into town and see if he could find a woman to take in the child. Thomas swung open the door confidently and marched inside.

His dusty, unkempt kitchen gleamed. The floors and window had been scrubbed, the ashes that had been piling up in the pail near the stove were gone, the furniture was dusted and the dishes were piled neatly in the cupboard. The curtains that Susannah had brought all the way from South Carolina were washed and hung in the window. In the middle of the table the oil lamp glowed, bathing the silverware in a soft yellow light. He never bothered to light the lamp when he ate dinner alone. In the middle of the room Kathleen lay on her stomach on a blanket, looking at herself in the shiny polished surface of a pot. Mattie was bent over the stove, frying salt pork in a cast iron pan. He had been planning to retrieve a clean shirt, some bread, and leftover meat and return to Johnny's cabin for the evening but the smells coming from the stove caused his stomach to rumble and the thought of a hot meal after a long day's work made his mouth water.

Mattie looked up at him and smiled, showing him a dimple. "Mr. Langley! I hope you'll join us for dinner."

Her smile sent a feeling of warmth over him that left him feeling unsure of himself and slightly off-kilter. Feeling foolish, he sat down quickly at the table and nodded curtly. Mattie chattered away to Kathleen while she poured Thomas a cup of coffee. Reaching for it, he took a large swallow then winced and spit it back in his cup.

Mattie looked at him, concerned. "Oh, dear. It's terrible, isn't it?"

"How much coffee did you put in the pot?" Thomas bellowed.

"I don't know! I can't remember! I've never made coffee before so I just kept adding coffee to the pot until it looked right," Mattie explained. "Mrs. Preston was always in charge of the kitchen and prepared the meals."

Thomas added two teaspoons of sugar and choked down a sip. At this rate, she'd use up his month's supply of coffee and sugar in a week.

"I can make another pot if you'd like," Mattie offered.

Thomas shook his head. "No need."

Mattie placed a plate of warm biscuits in the center of the table. Thomas reached for one eagerly. He took a bite and it disintegrated into sawdust in his mouth.

"I love a nice dry biscuit," Mattie told him. "Some people add so much lard in their biscuits it's like eating a piece of cake. I much prefer a nice dry biscuit."

Mattie knelt down on the floor beside Kathleen and rolled her onto her back. She tickled her stomach and the little girl kicked her legs and grasped at Mattie's face. She handed her a small square handkerchief which Kathleen clutched in one hand and touched with the other. She brought it to her mouth and chewed on it then withdrew it and studied it for a few seconds only to repeat the whole process over again.

Mattie placed two plates with generous helpings on the table. Quickly, Thomas cut into the salt pork and placed a small amount in his mouth. It was a little overcooked but he'd had worse. He dug into the potatoes eagerly.

"Your neighbor Alice Taylor stopped by this afternoon," Mattie began. Thomas nodded but said nothing. "Such a nice woman. Very kind and thoughtful. She invited me to the annual spring picnic on Sunday. I plan on taking Kathleen if that's alright with you," Mattie said. Thomas nodded silently again. "Of course, you could join us too. You may as well since you'll be in town anyway."

Thomas looked at her, confused. "Why will I be in town?"

"Well, you have to drive us, Mr. Langley. Even if I knew how to handle the team and wagon I haven't a single notion how to get to Boxwood. And walking is certainly out of the question. I can't very well carry Kathleen, all of her supplies, the dishes, and the food, can I?"

"Dishes? Food?" Thomas asked, panic rising. This picnic business was getting more complicated by the second. He sighed. "I don't have an entire day to spend in town waiting for you to finish eating and socializing. It's out of the question."

"I'm sure it won't take up an entire day. Just the morning and part of the afternoon," Mattie corrected.

Thomas' fist hit the table. "Listen, woman," he said harshly. "I hired you to tend to the child not travel about the countryside making friends and attending picnics."

Mattie's smile disappeared and her eyes narrowed. She pointed at him with her fork and leaned forward in her seat. "I assume, Mr. Langley, that "Listen, Woman" is a term of great respect wherever you come from and that is the reason you're using it to address me. I should warn you that is not the case in New York City and a less understanding woman would be offended. You, sir, should mind your manners."

Cowed, Thomas picked up his fork and shoveled a large helping of pork into his mouth. He chewed noisily and looked down at his plate.

Mattie settled back into her chair. "I was thinking that the picnic might be beneficial for both of us, Mr. Langley," she said amiably. "It might be good for the ladies in Boxwood to see what a sweet and lovely child Kathleen is because I heard from Mrs. Taylor this afternoon that Mrs. Petrie is going around town telling everyone that looking after Kathleen is a dreadful ordeal. Also, since you've repeatedly told me that my position here is only temporary, I had it in my mind to ask around about employment for myself. If you don't wish to come with us, Mr. and Mrs. Taylor said they would be glad to take us there and back."

Socks rose suddenly and barked loudly at the front door.

"Dog! Come!" Thomas ordered and pointed to his feet.

Socks ignored him. He barked louder and scratched at the door.

"Socks," Mattie called. The dog ran to her and sat quietly at her feet. "You can go out after we're done dinner." She gave him a pat on the head.

"So much for man's best friend," Thomas grumbled.

Mattie laughed. It was a deep, loud, hearty chuckle and it took all of Thomas' willpower to keep him from smiling. "Don't feel bad. I've been sneaking him pieces of meat under the table."

Socks left Mattie and ran to the door again, this time barking louder and scratching the door with greater urgency. Annoyed, Thomas set down his coffee and followed the dog to the door. He opened it and Socks bolted off the porch and ran, barking excitedly, into the darkness. The thick odor of smoke was unmistakable. Thomas looked to the left and saw a white cloud low in the field behind the barn. "The hay!" he yelled. "The hay's on fire!" He darted out of the house and ran toward the field.

Mattie had witnessed fire's devastating effects first hand. Fire was an ever-present danger in the overcrowded tenements and poorly built houses in her neighborhood. Families relied upon open flames for heat and light and even a moment of carelessness or inattention could result in an accident. As an assistant to Dr. Preston, Mattie had bandaged many burns and held the hands of countless victims who later succumbed to their injuries. *In New York there was at least a volunteer fire department*, Mattie thought. *But out here...* She could not sit idly in the house while Thomas battled the fire by himself. Mattie slipped on the sling she used to carry Kathleen and tucked the baby inside. Grabbing the milk pail beside the stove, she ran into the yard.

At the water pump she furiously worked the handle up and down, filling the pail with water. There was a bucket used for washing up beside the pump and she filled it too. Careful not to spill the water, Mattie ran toward the lean-to at the back of the barn where Thomas kept the hay.

Searching through the white curtain of smoke, Mattie saw Thomas near the door of the lean-to. He was pulling the stack apart with a pitchfork, stomping and kicking at it with his heavy boots in an effort to put out the smoldering fire. She tried not to breathe in the acrid smoke as she ran to him, handing him first one bucket of water then the other. Thomas poured the water on the hay and frantically handed her back the buckets. Smoke stung her eyes and settled in her chest as Mattie ran back to the pump. She coughed violently and sucked in a few breaths of fresh air. The smoke was worse than she'd anticipated. She thought that it would dissipate across the open prairie but it clung, low and heavy.

It was too dangerous to keep Kathleen with her, she decided. She made a move to take off the sling but looking down, she discovered that the little girl was snuggled closely into her chest, her eyes flickering open and shut peacefully. She pulled the sling up higher in the front, hoping to block out some of the smoke. Realizing that she needed some protection from the smoke too, Mattie felt for her petticoat under her skirt and, with both hands, ripped a strip of fabric from the bottom. She wet the cloth under the pump and covered her mouth and nose, tying it tightly at the back of her head. Filling the buckets, she ran as fast as she could into the field to find Thomas.

They worked together in a frenzied attempt to control the fire. If the fire managed to get into the barn there would be no stopping it and it was unlikely that they could free the animals before the fire consumed them. Finally, the hay lay black and sooty on the dirt floor of the lean-to. Mattie collapsed beside the barn and swept her hair back from her eyes, dragging a dirty hand across her forehead. She peeked inside the sling and found to her great relief that Kathleen had fallen asleep. Breathing hard, Thomas sat down beside her, exhausted.

"If hay is too wet and the pile is too thick it can heat up and light on fire," he explained to her. "But this hay is dry and already piled. It's been there since last summer. It shouldn't have ignited. That wasn't like any haystack fire I've ever seen. Almost no flame, just a lot of smoke." He gestured to the barn and lean-to. "No damage to either building."

Mattie sat up. "You're not saying that someone tried to burn your hay on purpose?"

Thomas shrugged. "Don't know. I guess it doesn't really matter. I've still got a barn but now that hay's no good for animal feed." Thomas briefly looked at Mattie then looked away. "You kept a cool head instead of running around crying and carrying on," he said brusquely.

Mattie smiled and shook her head. "Where are you from, Mr. Langley, that when disaster strikes all of the women run around wringing their hands and crying? It's my experience that women are much tougher and bolder than that."

"Some, maybe," Thomas conceded. He looked as though he might speak again then hesitated. Mattie looked at him expectantly. "I suppose it would be alright to call me Thomas. That is if you feel it's appropriate."

"Then you must call me Mattie," she said.

Thomas nodded. The crisp night air enveloped them, two small dots on the immense prairie. They sat in companionable silence, the only sounds coming from the swaying grasses and the small insects that flitted about in the darkness. Mattie had never seen a more beautiful sky, had never seen brighter stars. Even though things hadn't turned out the way she'd expected when she arrived in Boxwood, she knew she would never return to New York City. It would be impossible to leave the Dakota Territory now; she'd fallen in love with its remote peacefulness. Maybe one day she'd find a man who would be willing to make a life with her here.

Next to her, Kathleen wriggled and opened her eyes. Mattie trailed a finger across her brows. "This little miss has finished her usual forty-five minute sleep. I must take her back to the house before she catches a chill. I'll leave a washbasin on the porch for you to wash in, if you'd like."

"That'd be much appreciated," Thomas said without meeting her eyes.

CHAPTER SIX

Mattie struggled to open her eyes against the bright early morning sunshine streaming in through the parlor's small window. Overwhelming fatigue urged her to close them and return to sleep but she knew she wouldn't have much time to herself before Kathleen woke up. She looked over at the pad of blankets where Kathleen was sleeping. One chubby pink hand rested near her face while she sucked on the thumb of the opposite hand. Mattie quietly sifted through her trunk of belongings and came up with a plain brown work dress. She dressed and combed her hair then closed the parlor door so her work in the kitchen wouldn't wake Kathleen. She lit the stove, put water on for coffee and popped the loaf of bread she'd left to rise the night before into the oven.

With the change to goat's milk, Kathleen had stopped throwing up every time she ate but her sleeping patterns hadn't improved. The baby screamed and cried for an hour to two hours then fell into an exhausted and restless sleep for forty-five minutes only to wake up and start the whole cycle all over again. Mattie rocked her, held her, sang to her, carried her around in the sling and walked up and down the stairs and from one room to the next, all to no avail. The little girl could not be consoled. As night turned to day, Mattie found her patience fading and several times had to leave Kathleen laying on the blankets screaming while she went onto the porch to calm herself.

Mattie washed her face and hands and deftly wove her hair into a neat braid. She'd seen many women sick from exhaustion while caring for a colicky baby and she knew she would need to sleep when Kathleen slept but she wanted to get a few tasks out of the way too. The night before, when Kathleen had been thrashing and moving about on the blankets, Mattie knew she had to find somewhere safe for the baby to sleep. She had already examined the loft and knew there was nothing of any use upstairs and the drawers in the cabinet in the parlor were too small and shallow to be used as a bed. While putting spoonfuls of coffee into the pot her gaze traveled to the barn. *Perhaps there is a box or crate in the barn that could be used as a cradle,* Mattie thought.

After checking on Kathleen, she slipped outside and hurried across the yard.

The horses and goat flicked their ears in acknowledgment and the sow grunted as she fed her ten little piglets. Like the house, the barn too was sparse but just past the pig pen Mattie spied a large table laid out with woodworking tools. She reached out to examine them but they were organized so precisely that she quickly withdrew her hand. A torn white and green quilt peeked out from under the table. Mattie stuck her hand under the quilt and grasped a smooth piece of wood. Thinking that she'd found a crate, she dragged the heavy wooden object into the light.

It was a beautiful cradle, ornately carved just like the porch. It rocked on two perfectly balanced rockers and had been stained and painstakingly polished to a shine. At the head of the cradle written in script was the name Matthew.

"What are you doing with that?" Thomas' deep voice yelled from behind her.

Mattie spun around in surprise. "I was trying to find something for Kathleen to sleep in and I stumbled upon this," she gestured to the cradle.

"Put it away," Thomas said, his voice hard.

"I'm sorry. I seem to have upset you," Mattie said.

"Put it away, woman." Thomas repeated every word slowly and deliberately.

Mattie pushed the cradle back under the bench and covered it with the quilt. She stood up slowly. "Kathleen needs somewhere to sleep. Perhaps when you go into town tomorrow you could inquire about purchasing or borrowing a cradle for her." Mattie walked past him toward the barn door then stopped. She knew she should keep walking, go back into the house and mind her own business but she also knew it was against her nature to turn away from someone in so much pain. "Matthew was your son?"

Thomas stood silently for so long Mattie thought he was ignoring her. "He was born on our way out here. He came too early and did not live. He's buried beside the Missouri River."

"I am so sorry, Thomas." Mattie gently laid a hand on his arm. It was meant to be a gesture of kindness, of compassion and comfort but the feel of his skin against her palm sent a flush of heat through her body. Unnerved at her reaction, she withdrew her hand and tucked it behind her back.

"It was my fault," he confessed bitterly. "I pushed Susannah to leave South Carolina that spring even though I knew she was with child because I didn't want to wait another year before heading west. If I had thought of someone other than myself...if I had thought of the dangers...well, Matthew would still be here."

"You don't know that, Thomas," Mattie said. "You may have stayed in South Carolina and he may have come too early anyway. Even a healthy and careful mother can lose a baby. Sometimes you do everything right and it still turns out wrong"

"What do you know of it?" Thomas spat out angrily.

Mattie winced. "It is true; I've never been lucky enough to have a child. But I have held countless mothers who lost theirs and felt despair and emptiness overtake their bodies. And I have had children breathe their last ragged breaths in my arms. Just because I have never borne a child doesn't mean I have never felt the pain of a child's passing." With that, she turned and marched back into the house, careful to square her shoulders and stare straight ahead. She would not let him see how much he had hurt her.

Thomas did not arrive at the house for the noon meal and as it grew closer to suppertime Mattie feared that he would not show up at the house again. *When will I learn to hold my tongue?* Kathleen asked herself. *Mrs. Preston was always after me to stop my constant opinionated prattling.* As she finished feeding Kathleen and was about to start her own supper she heard Thomas' heavy boots on the front porch. The door flew open and he walked in carrying the cradle. Mutely, he set it down near the stove and sat heavily in his chair.

Mattie beamed. "It's wonderful, Thomas. Kathleen will love it."

Thomas sat down at the table and poured himself a cup of coffee. Cautiously he tasted it and, finding it much improved from the day before, drank it.

"Here, hold Kathleen," Mattie said, handing him the baby. "I want to get the cradle ready for her so she can lay in it while we eat dinner."

Thomas waved the child away. "Put her on the floor. I'm drinking coffee."

"If I put her down she's likely to cry. Just put the coffee down," Mattie told him.

Thomas sighed and put his coffee cup on the table. He held the little girl at arm's length stiffly, one hand on her back and the other across her chest.

Mattie shook her head. "Why are you holding her like that? She's not a bag of grain you're trying to throw over your shoulder." She pushed Kathleen closer to him and adjusted his hands. Touching him, Mattie again felt a surge of heat run from her hand to her face. She quickly brought her hand back to her sides.

"She's going to fall," Thomas grumbled.

"If you keep holding her she's not going to fall," Mattie told him.

"What about her head and neck? I think I'm holding her arms too tightly."

Mattie laughed. "Honestly, Thomas. She's fine."

Mattie left the room and went to collect the blankets in the parlor. Gazing at them from the doorway of the parlor, she could see that Thomas loved Kathleen deeply but she also sensed in him a reluctance to become too attached to her, as if she might be snatched away from him at any moment. Mattie took her time finding the blankets, knowing that as soon as she returned to the kitchen Thomas would want to put the baby in the cradle. She wanted him to hold his daughter for as long as possible.

Thomas looked into Kathleen's bright eyes. Gently, he brushed his finger against her smooth, pink skin. She grabbed his nose and felt his face, smiling and making little gurgling noises. She was so small and so perfect. He never wanted to do anything that would hurt her. She needed so much but he had so little to offer. He didn't know the first thing about raising a child. How could he ever give her the life she deserved? How would he keep her safe in a place like the Dakota Territory?

Sunday morning Mattie bustled around the kitchen, making the picnic lunch and gathering the supplies Kathleen would need for the morning. After dressing Kathleen in a long flowing muslin gown, Mattie put on her best dress, a dark blue linen gown with finely tatted lace on the sleeves that Mrs. Preston had made for her to wear on her wedding day. She had washed her hair the night before and she brushed it thoroughly and pinned it into a high knot, leaving a cascade of curls at the back. She adjusted her hat in the small mirror in the parlor.

Though he'd said nothing about taking her to the picnic, Thomas put on a clean shirt and silently readied the wagon for the drive to town. He seemed more brooding than usual so Mattie concentrated on admiring the peaceful, yet wild landscape around her. As they turned down the main street and began to approach the general store Mattie's stomach turned anxiously. She didn't know anyone except Alice. She was unsure if she was welcome or what the other residents would think of her. Would they judge her because she'd come to Boxwood to be a mail order bride? Would they think she was behaving inappropriately by staying in Thomas' house to care for his daughter? She took a deep breath and tried to calm herself.

Thomas pulled the wagon into the livery and began unloading the baskets of food and the supplies. When he headed for the lane to the right of the store, Mattie followed along with Kathleen on her hip. Behind the store people were milling about, some setting down blankets, others talking in small groups. Thomas dropped the baskets on the grass next to several other baskets of food.

"I'll be at the hotel," he told her and stalked off in the direction of the main street.

Timidly, Mattie scanned the crowd. She saw Alice who waved and smiled. Mattie went to join her.

"I'm so glad you came," Alice said, giving her arm a squeeze.

"Thank you so much for inviting me," Mattie said.

"You must meet my husband," she gestured to the man standing beside her, a tall thin man with a head of brown curls. "This is Will."

"Miss Robinson, it is a pleasure," Will said, taking her hand.

"I'm very pleased to meet you. You must call me Mattie," she smiled at him.

"My wife hasn't stopped talking about you since her visit. She told me you're a wonder with children. I see you've managed to get this little one to stop crying," Will gestured to Kathleen.

"You're too kind. She stills cries a lot but she's coming along," Mattie said.

"Well, we're very happy that you're here in Boxwood. We might have need of your advice in a few months," Will said, looking at Alice with a shy, loving smile. Jealousy welled up inside Mattie, hot and biting. She longed so desperately for someone to look at her like that. "You are staying, aren't you?"

"I hope so. I really like it here but Mr. Langley is very adamant that my position looking after Kathleen is only temporary," Mattie said.

Alice waved a hand. "The man would be a fool to part with you."

"Is he treating you alright? Langley is miserable on his best day, loathsome on his worst," Will said. "I don't know how you put up with him. I wouldn't sell him a horse I didn't like."

"Will!" Alice admonished.

"Alright, my wife. You're right. That is terribly unkind of me to say. Let's talk of more pleasant things. Mattie, if I may be so bold to bring up the subject, I know of several eligible bachelors who have asked about you," Will said.

"Oh my goodness," Mattie blushed.

"I'd be more than happy to introduce you," he offered.

"You came all this way to marry. Now that you're here, why not choose a husband for yourself? I'm certainly not speaking ill of the dead but there are many men in Boxwood who are better prospects than John Stark. First of all, he had to be nearing a hundred," Alice said.

Will laughed. "My lovely wife is prone to exaggeration. Johnny was in his fifties."

"Well, he looked like he was a hundred. He rarely bathed and he cursed constantly," Alice said.

"He was an old army scout," Will explained. "He was a little rough around the edges."

Looking past Mattie, Alice smiled and waved. "There's Clara and Louisa." Two women, one a short, petite blonde with glasses and the other a thin, dark-haired woman, waved back and headed toward Alice.

"I can see that I'm soon to be outnumbered," Will said. "I'll go join the men." He kissed his wife gently on the top of the head and headed toward a group of men standing in a circle.

The two women approached Mattie and Alice. "Mattie, I'd like to introduce you to Clara Gibson and Louisa Duncan. Clara is our schoolmistress."

The petite blonde smiled kindly. "It's not much of a school, I'm afraid. I only have five students."

"You poor dear," Louisa started. "Stuck day and night in that house with that horrible ogre Thomas Langley."

"We're certainly not stuck in the house together," Mattie blushed. "He spends most of his days in the fields and he spends his nights in Mr. Stark's cabin."

Louisa put a hand on her arm. "I wasn't suggesting anything inappropriate. Me and my big mouth! Please forgive me."

"You'll get used to Louisa's brashness," Clara laughed. "Eventually."

"Richard is always telling me to think before I speak but

after a lifetime of saying whatever comes into my mind I'm not likely to change," Louisa said.

"And Richard wouldn't have it any other way," Alice told her.

Louisa turned to Mattie. "We must get together. I have a little boy that I'm desperately trying to teach to hold a spoon properly but I'm having no luck whatsoever. I heard from Alice that you know a great deal about children. Maybe you'd have some words of wisdom?"

"That's very flattering. I don't know if I'd be of any help but I'll try," Mattie told her.

"Really, it's just an excuse to go visiting. Some days I just need to talk to another adult so badly!" Louisa laughed.

"Clara, are you eating with us? Or will you be eating with a certain young gentleman?" Alice asked playfully.

Clara turned bright red. "I will be eating with Joshua."

Alice and Louisa giggled.

"You two are terrible," Clara said.

"Joshua Ainsley is courting Clara. He runs the telegraph office," Alice explained to her.

"And he's very handsome," Louisa added.

"Louisa!" Clara gasped.

Several older women who looked to be in charge began taking food out of the baskets and setting it up on long planks laying across sawhorses.

"Our blanket's already set up over here," Alice said. She grabbed Mattie's arm as if they were old friends and steered her over to a blue and yellow quilt that was spread out on the grass. Mattie smiled broadly. She couldn't help it. It had been years since she'd had a good friend, a real confidant. There was Rose Bennett, who did charity work in the neighborhood but she was more of an acquaintance than a friend. She came from a wealthy family and certainly wouldn't expect to be friends with someone like Mattie. All of Mattie's childhood friends went into service and moved away or were married and no longer had the time to spend socializing. Mattie sat down on the blanket and tucked Kathleen into the crook of her arm. Will soon joined them, sitting Mattie and Alice's baskets of plates, cups, and silverware on the blanket.

A heavyset man got up and smiled at the small group. "Good morning. We're all standing here so that means we made it through another devil of a Dakota winter." A few cheers rang out from the crowd. "Let's all take this time to visit with our neighbors, talk about all the latest news and eat some mighty good food. Clarence, I heard that Mrs. Telford made her delicious apple pie again this year but we're limiting you to one piece." The crowd laughed and a short thin man standing in a group of older men turned bright red and let out a loud snort.

Mattie couldn't stop smiling. In the short time she'd been in Boxwood she felt more accepted and at home than she'd ever felt in New York City. She hoped desperately that she could find a way to stay.

CHAPTER SEVEN

The pile of soiled laundry loomed large in a corner of the upstairs loft where Mattie had been tucking it out of sight since her arrival at the farm. Laundry was her least favorite job but with the day's warm sunshine and light spring breeze she knew she could have everything washed, dried and put away by dinner time. Kathleen was sleeping peacefully on the porch, making it the perfect time to set up her buckets by the pump and begin the arduous task. Groaning, Mattie carried the basket of dirty clothes and diapers outside. She walked around the corner of the house and stopped.

Thomas was bent over under the pump, his back to her. Rivulets of water ran down his broad shirtless back and shoulders. The left side of his back was a mess of puckered, uneven skin and deep divots. Rough scars that had faded to a silvery white ran haphazardly from his neck to his waist and spread down his left arm. Mattie gasped and dropped her laundry basket. Thomas turned around and growled. Mattie's breath caught and she felt her face redden at the sight of his hard, muscled chest, a faint trail of light brown hair disappearing into his waistband. His pants sat low across his taut stomach revealing a mass of scar tissue across his hip. Hastily, Thomas grabbed his shirt and threw it on, covering his wet body. His back to her, he buttoned it quickly.

"I'm sorry," Mattie stammered. White hot heat seared her face. "Please forgive me...I didn't know you were here." She looked down at the ground.

"I thought you were in the house," Thomas mumbled. He shoved his hat back on his head and turned to leave.

"Did you get those in the war?" Mattie asked.

Thomas nodded but looked away from her. "A shell landed nearby and a barn exploded. I caught shrapnel in my back and leg mostly but a few smaller pieces hit me in the face and neck."

"I'm sure you were in a great deal of pain. I heard that the Confederacy had very few trained doctors."

"Never saw a doctor. A couple of Union soldiers found me and put me into a railway car headed to Camp Douglas. The other prisoners tried the best they could to fix me up but we had no supplies; no clean water, no threat, no bandages except what we could make from our own clothes."

"You were a prisoner of war?" Mattie said softly.

"For more than two years" Thomas answered bitterly.

"Your back," Mattie gestured. "Does it hurt?"

Thomas shrugged. "Only when I think about it." He shifted uncomfortably. "And I try not to think about it." He nodded without meeting her eyes and walked off in the direction of the barn.

She was repulsed by him. Thomas watched the basket of laundry fall and saw Mattie's face as she looked away, her eyes refusing to meet his while her hands nervously swept the clothes back into the basket. He hadn't looked at his back in several years but he doubted time had improved it. The large, jagged scars that formed a rough and twisted braid of skin along his leg and hip hadn't improved though he noticed over the last year that they had begun to change from an angry red to a silvery white. Thomas walked angrily past the barn and turned left toward the river. What did he care what a babbling spinster from New York thought of him?

Thomas found his cattle grazing lazily in the back pasture. His herd was small but would be profitable. He had thirty calves that would be going to market and several older heifers. A young cow came up to him and rubbed his shoulder with her nose. He gave her head a strong rub and patted her neck. Cattle were so much easier to deal with than people. He scanned the field and counted his herd. Thomas noticed with a start that his bull was missing. He strode through the grass, searching for a hint of the bull's pointed horns but saw none. Though he could get ornery, the bull usually didn't stray far from his herd of females.

Thomas followed a worn path to the riverbank where several heifers were cooling themselves in the mud and laying in the long grass with their calves. He walked several feet from the rest of the herd along the bank and looked out across the fast-moving water. The large bull was across the river on a flat piece of higher ground, lying on his side, legs extended. Thomas strode through the waist deep water and bent down to examine him. He was already beginning to bloat even though the morning air was cool. Dried mud covered his legs and underbelly. Thomas patted his head. He must have become stuck in the mud, panicked and drowned.

Thomas sighed. Losing his only bull meant he couldn't grow his herd now unless he kept one of the male calves and then it would be more than a year before he would be capable of producing any offspring. Another setback. Cursing under his breath, he waded back out of the water and headed to the barn to grab a shovel.

CHAPTER EIGHT

In the middle of the week Mattie looked up from the stove to see a familiar wagon stop in front of the house. Alice and Clara hopped out and waved.

"Would you care to sit inside?" Mattie asked as the pair climbed the stairs to the porch. "Perhaps in the parlor?"

Alice made a face. "We have all winter to sit inside. Let's sit on the porch."

"I just finished baking a cake. Would you care for some?" Mattie asked.

Alice shook her head. "None for me, thank you."

"Nor I. Mrs. Fisher served a rather large noon meal and I couldn't eat another bite," Clara said, sitting primly on one of the chairs brought out to the porch from the kitchen.

"You're both passing up cake? Is my baking that terrible?" Mattie asked, a smile playing at her lips.

"It's awful," laughed Alice. "But we didn't come here for your baking."

"We have more important things to discuss than cake," Clara said excitedly. "After the picnic, Joshua and I were talking and we both thought you'd be an excellent match for his brother, Alec." Seeing Mattie shift uncomfortably in her chair, Clara grabbed her hand. "Before you say no, just listen," she told her. "He's a perfect gentleman. He has a homestead just outside of town. He can be rather quiet but he's incredibly witty."

"And very handsome. Goodness, but that man is handsome! Though, not as handsome as my Will," Alice added quickly.

"Handsome?" Mattie said. She shook her head. "I don't think he'd be interested in me, then. I'm not a woman most handsome men want to be seen with."

Alice rolled her eyes. "Please! Any man, handsome or homely, would want to get his hands on those curves."

The women shrieked with laughter.

"Alice! That is positively scandalous!" Clara blushed. She turned to Mattie. "Alec gets all sorts of grand ideas but doesn't take anything seriously. He roams around constantly, from Chicago to the Dakotas to Mexico to Bolivia and goodness knows where and back to the Dakotas. It drives Joshua completely mad with worry. He's owned his homestead for two years and hardly spent more than a few months there. We keep telling him a man can't spend his life living like a vagabond. We thought that maybe if he had a good woman, a worldly woman from New York City, maybe he'd settle down. It would be good for him. And for you."

"I hadn't thought about meeting any gentlemen," Mattie told the women truthfully.

"Oh, say yes," Clara begged. "I think you'd really like him."

Mattie hesitated then quickly relented. Instead of relying on others to map out her future, she finally had the opportunity to take control of her own life. She would be a fool to waste this chance. "I suppose there wouldn't be any harm in meeting him."

Clara clapped her hands. "Wonderful!"

"Will and I are going into town on Saturday. We'll stop by and pick you up," Alice said.

"And I've already made arrangements with Joshua. He'll make sure Alec is in town. I'll perform the introductions and then suggest we all go for tea at the hotel."

"I'll have Kathleen with me," Mattie reminded the women. "He won't mind?"

"Not one bit," Clara said.

"And if she gets a little fussy you just pass her to me. I need all the practice I can get calming a fussy baby," Alice said.

"It seems you two have thought of everything," Mattie laughed. Suddenly remembering Thomas' hasty mutterings over breakfast that morning, Mattie turned to Alice. "Thomas was just saying this morning that he's planning to go into town on Saturday. I'll ride in with him."

"Alec is going to be thrilled. You're really going to like him," Clara assured her.

But will he like me? Mattie wondered.

Saturday morning dawned clear and bright without a cloud in the sky. Mattie took extra time with her hair, braiding it and pinning it up in the back like she'd seen in the fashion papers in New York City. She pressed her best blue dress and fussed with her hat.

"The wagon's ready," Thomas announced from the kitchen.

Mattie entered the kitchen from the parlor and Thomas eyed her strangely. "What?" she asked.

"You did something...to your hair," he muttered.

"I felt like dressing up a little today," Mattie said, trying to sound aloof.

Thomas shrugged and handed her Kathleen. "Seems like a lot of work just for a visit into town."

Ignoring his comment, she set Kathleen on a hip and grabbed her reticule with a free hand. Mattie nuzzled the little girl's neck and she giggled and clapped her hands together.

The wagon creaked and lurched over the uneven prairie toward Boxwood. Thomas sat silently guiding the horses, only making the occasional noise to urge them forward or steer them clear of a muddy spot. Mattie talked and sang to Kathleen and sat her on her lap to point out butterflies and a fat prairie dog that scurried beside the wagon. Just as he had the week before, Thomas drove the wagon to the livery and scrambled out to tend to his horses before one of the stable boys could offer.

"Mattie!" a familiar voice called out. Mattie turned around and saw Clara, Joshua and a second man approaching. Her stomach flipped nervously.

"Here, let me help you with the baby." Clara held out her hands.

As Mattie made a motion to disembark, the man standing beside Joshua took off his hat and held out his hand. "M'am," he said politely. Taking off his hat he grinned mischievously with a perfect row of white teeth, his deep green eyes scanning her from head to toe. He smoothed his blonde hair before setting his hat back on his head at a jaunty angle.

Mattie took his hand and smiled. "Thank you."

"What a surprise, Mattie!" Clara said. "I had absolutely no idea you were coming into town today. Whatever are you doing here? I don't think you've been introduced to Joshua's brother, Mr. Alec Ainsley."

Alec took her hand and bowed.

"I'm pleased to meet you," Mattie said.

"It's a pleasure to meet you, Miss Robinson. Clara has talked about you non-stop since we called on her this morning. What a coincidence that we should meet up with you," he said, a smile playing at the corners of his mouth.

"I'm not sure it's such a coincidence," Mattie answered, smiling back. "Saturday is a popular day for shopping." She reached out for Kathleen who had begun to wiggle and whimper in Clara's arms. Finding herself in familiar hands, the baby calmed down and looked out at everyone, one fist in her mouth and another in Mattie's hair.

The loud clatter of horse tackle interrupted their conversation. Thomas stood impatiently beside the wagon, arms crossed, his eyes dark.

"Mr. Langley, how do you do, sir?" Joshua said politely.

"Fine," Thomas answered gruffly. "I'm leaving in an hour," he said to Mattie and stomped off.

"I see Mr. Langley is as pleasant as always," Joshua commented.

"Never mind him. Mattie, weren't you saying the other day that you just couldn't wait to try the tea at the hotel dining room?" Clara asked loudly. "You're in town now and I know I'm feeling a little parched. Let's all go have tea at the hotel. Together. Joshua, isn't that a good idea?" Clara linked her arm through Joshua's and scurried across the road and onto the wooden sidewalk, careful to keep Joshua several steps ahead of Mattie and Alec.

"I must apologize, Miss Robinson," Alec began.

Mattie smiled slyly. "Is the tea at the hotel that bad, Mr. Ainsley? Or perhaps you're apologizing for Clara's feeble attempt to make it seem like our meeting wasn't an intricately planned and much discussed event."

"She is a terrible actress, isn't she?" he laughed. "I'm afraid Clara has misled you. She and my brother are convinced I'm in need of a wife and have decided to throw themselves wholeheartedly into the search for the future Mrs. Alec Ainsley," Alec said.

"And you have no interest in marrying," Mattie finished.

"I'm not opposed to marriage," he assured her. "One day. Maybe. There are a lot of things I want to do before I get tied down with a wife and children."

"Clara mentioned that you were a bit of a traveler," Mattie said.

He laughed. "She would say that. I'm trying to start my own horse ranch. The army is going to need good horses in these parts, not to mention all the settlers who have started coming out here. I think I could become a very wealthy man."

"You're very ambitious, Mr. Ainsley," she told him.

"It seems to me like it's the right time to have a bit of ambition. This territory is just getting started; men like my brother and I, even Thomas Langley, are going to decide what type of place this is going to be."

"And what about women?" Mattie asked. "We have no part to play?"

"I can't imagine life without women. I'm very fond of them," Alec smiled charmingly.

Mattie blushed and looked away, flustered by his boldness. "Honestly, you needn't feel obliged to come to tea. I won't be offended if you want to leave."

Alec stopped. "I said I wasn't interested in a wife. I didn't say I wasn't interested in spending some time with an interesting woman."

Mattie stopped beside him and stared him down coldly. "I'm sure there's a saloon or a hotel nearby full of interesting women you could spend time with, if that's what you're after."

He held his hands up in defense. "You've misunderstood, Miss Robinson. I just meant that maybe we could take a stroll together or go on a picnic. I think we would enjoy each other's company. Does it have to be more complicated than that?"

"I may have come to Boxwood as a mail-order bride but I'm not a whore, Mr. Ainsley and I won't put up with anything less than gentlemanly behavior."

Alec offered her his elbow. "Of course, Miss Robinson. I would never think otherwise."

Alec Ainsley? Thomas thought angrily. That dandy? He changed into a three-piece suit every time he went into town. And he was boring, incredibly boring. Thomas once listened to him droned on and on for forty-five minutes about the complexity of a horse's fetlock. Mattie couldn't really be thinking of him as a potential husband, could she? Is that why she fixed her hair differently and fussed with her clothes the entire way to town?

He steeled himself. It didn't matter. If Mattie wanted to marry that tiresome bore then that was her own business. He just couldn't picture a woman like Mattie, a woman so quick and vibrant, with a man like that. *Just who do you picture her marrying?* He taunted himself cruelly. *You?*

CHAPTER NINE

The following week Thomas was hitching the horses to the wagon when Mattie stepped out onto the porch to dump a pail of dirty dishwater.

"Are you going somewhere?" she called.

"Sheriff Bradshaw is supposed to be back today. I'm going to talk to him about the fire," Thomas said, swinging up into the seat.

"Wait just a moment and I'll go with you. I want to talk to Mrs. Bradshaw," Mattie said.

Thomas sighed, put out. "All right. But I'm not waiting for an hour while you get all prettied up."

"It would take me more than an hour to look pretty, I'm afraid. You'd be waiting forever," Mattie laughed as she ducked back into the house.

What did she mean by that? Thomas wondered during the drive to town. No, he thought, she wasn't pretty. That was a word that described flowers and women's hats; it didn't describe Mattie. He thought about the delicate white curve of her neck that he'd noticed for the first time the day before when her hair was pinned up. The wagon jerked forward sharply and Mattie reached out instinctively to steady herself. He looked down at the long, delicate fingers splayed across his arm. Apologizing, she pulled her hand away and straightened her skirts. Thomas wondered about the long legs hidden under those skirts. His eyes settled on her voluptuous hips before he could stop himself. He swallowed hard and gazed straight ahead fixing his eyes on the silhouette of Boxwood in the distance. No, Mattie Robinson wasn't pretty. She was something else entirely.

After inquiring at the Sheriff's office, Thomas was told that the Sheriff and Mrs. Bradshaw were at home. Their little white clapboard house stood alone at the very end of Boxwood's main street surrounded on three sides by a field of grass that was just beginning to sprout dots of color from the blooming prairie wildflowers. Before Thomas had even stopped the horses, the front door flew open and a thin older woman wearing a pair of men's pants and a neatly fitted cotton shirt stepped outside. Her light brown hair flowed freely down her back to her waist. Mattie gazed at her, enthralled.

"You must be Matilda!" Dora Bradshaw's voice boomed.

"I prefer Mattie," she answered as she climbed down from the wagon. "I'm so very glad to meet you, ma'am."

"And I prefer Dora," the woman answered back. "You must accept my apologies. You poor girl, you came all the way out here only to find that Mr. Stark had already passed months before. Then, to make matters worse, I wasn't even here to greet you. What a mess!"

Mattie patted the woman's hand. "There is nothing to apologize for. It was a misunderstanding, a mix up with the mail."

"Well, I'm very glad to see you were able to find someone to take you in," Dora eyed Thomas.

"Nice to see you again, Dora," Thomas said.

"Mr. Langley was kind enough to give me a job looking after his daughter until I figure out what to do next," Mattie said.

"Yes, I heard all about it. You've become the talk of the town," Dora told her. Seeing Mattie's panicked expression she hastily clarified, "Not for any scandalous reasons, I assure you my dear. You've become the talk of the town because you managed to get this little girl to stop crying." She wiggled her fingers at Kathleen who had since awakened and was looking out of the sling fastened around Mattie's shoulder.

Thomas cleared his throat. "I came to speak to the Sheriff."

"Yes, of course," Dora said. "He's out back." She turned to Mattie. "Come inside and we'll visit in the parlor."

Thomas left to find the Sheriff and Mattie followed Dora into the little house. The cozy parlor was decorated with tintypes and treasures, two comfortable chairs and a settee lined with decorative pillows. Dora moved a ball of wool and some knitting needles from the settee to a basket filled with finished socks and mittens. "You'll find out that winter's mighty long and as cold as the devil around here. The Sheriff and I take those up to the Indian Reservation. It helps a bit," she explained.

Mattie sat down on the settee and took Kathleen out of the sling.

"May I hold her?" Dora asked.

"Certainly." Mattie handed Kathleen to Dora. The baby kicked and fussed then began to cry. Dora turned Kathleen around so she faced outward and could see Mattie. Though she still wriggled uncomfortably, the little girl stopped crying. Mattie stroked Kathleen's head gently and smiled at her. "You're all right."

"She's really quite taken with you," Dora observed.

"I think she just really needed some attention and affection," Mattie said.

"And Mr. Langley seems quite taken with you as well," Dora told her.

"Thomas?" Mattie shook her head. "Thomas is not taken with me, I assure you. He tolerates me, I suppose, but I'm sure that's more out of necessity."

"Well, you're the only one he tolerates, my dear. Perhaps he'll keep you on as a nanny or housekeeper," Dora suggested.

"He's adamant that this is only a temporary situation," Mattie said.

Dora rolled her eyes and waved a hand impatiently in the air. "A temporary situation? My goodness, does he think that one day a few weeks from now the baby will just wake up and be able to care for herself? That's a man for you."

"Even if it wasn't temporary, it would never work," Mattie pointed out. "Thomas can't very well go on living in Mr. Stark's cabin until Kathleen is grown. And he can't stay in the house with me. It wouldn't be proper."

"That is true. Though there is a rather easy solution that would solve everyone's problems."

Mattie raised an eyebrow. "What solution is that?"

"Marry Mr. Langley," Dora told her.

Mattie chuckled loudly. "I don't think so. I mean, he's so...he's just...so very…"

"Grouchy?" Dora suggested. "Angry? Surly?"

"Broken," Mattie finished. She sighed. "He's so very broken and I'm not sure I can fix him."

"Maybe not everything that's broken needs to be fixed. I've got a dozen tea cups without handles but I can still drink out of them," Dora said gently.

"But without a handle you'll burn your hands if the tea's too hot. And I don't want to burn my hands," Mattie answered quietly.

Dora nodded and the two women sat quietly playing with Kathleen for a few minutes.

"What do you think of Alec Ainsley?" Mattie asked suddenly, impulsively.

Dora sat forward and grinned. "Well, well. Alec Ainsley. Has he come forward as a prospective suitor?"

Mattie smiled shyly. "I'm not really sure what he is, to tell you the truth. We were introduced last Saturday. He's really very charming and quite funny. He asked to call on me this Wednesday afternoon."

"I've never found the man to be interested in much unless you want to talk about horses, then he'll talk your ear off. But he's young and a hard worker with a nice homestead. And it doesn't hurt that he's darned handsome," Dora said, laughing.

"That smile!" Mattie giggled. "He certainly could charm any woman with that grin of his!"

She caught a slight movement out of the corner of her eye. Mattie turned to see Thomas leaning against the door to the parlor, his arms crossed. His face was stone, an expressionless mask but his eyes blazed. How long had he been standing there? How much of her conversation had he heard? Mattie looked back at Kathleen and Dora, mortified.

"Time to go. I've got work to do," he said gruffly.

CHAPTER TEN

Mattie stood up for the fifth time to retrieve an item she'd forgotten to put on the table. When she sat down she bumped her plate, knocking a fork to the floor. She bent down to retrieve it and hit her head against the table. Rubbing her forehead, she sat back against her chair and sighed. "I don't know what's wrong with me."

"You seem nervous," Thomas said, trying to sound casual.

"That's ridiculous. Why would I be nervous? Mr. Ainsley is just stopping by for a few hours to talk and perhaps take a walk. That's nothing to be nervous about," Mattie told him.

"I forgot Ainsley was coming by today," Thomas lied. He looked down and ate the rest of his meal in silence.

He wasn't spying on Mattie and Alec, Thomas told himself later that afternoon. It just happened to be a perfect day to finally tackle all the odd jobs around the house that he'd been putting off. Thomas was bent over hacking a patch of brambles with a scythe along the side of the house when Alec rode up in a new buggy pulled by two large black horses. He stopped just outside the front door and jumped down nimbly, his polished leather shoes hitting the dirt.

He touched the brim of his fashionable straw hat with its wide red ribbon. "Good day, Mr. Langley," Alec greeted Thomas warmly. He straightened his vest and brushed the dust from his cream-colored linen suit.

"Ainsley," Thomas responded without looking up from the patch of brambles. Ridiculous. The man looked like he was dressed for a garden party at a city park.

Alec looked past Thomas and into the paddock where Thomas' three horses were grazing on grass. His eyes lit up. "Well, well, well," he whistled, eyeing the smallest of Thomas' horses. "Isn't she something." Alec leaned up against the paddock rails and craned his head forward, examining the sturdy little mare. "Do you mind if I get a closer look?"

Thomas shrugged. "Suit yourself." He smirked. The little mare didn't take well to strangers and he knew that she'd buck and bite anyone who got close. It had taken months of coaxing before she'd let Thomas stand in the corral.

Excitedly, Alec grabbed onto the top rail of the fence and swung his legs over. The sound of his shoes hitting the dirt startled the mare and she neighed and stamped her feet uneasily. Alec approached the horse slowly making low, comforting sounds and keeping his arms wide. He stopped about ten feet from her but continued making the soft noises. It took fifteen minutes but the mare gradually stepped close enough to Alec that he could touch her. He rubbed her neck and scratched behind her ears.

"This is a Choctaw Indian pony, isn't it? I've never seen a real one; just pictures of them in books. Where did you find her?" Alistair asked.

"She wandered in here last winter after a real bad snowstorm," Thomas answered.

"What a stroke of luck. She's a rare beauty. I don't suppose you'd sell her? I'm trying to start up my own herd and she's just what I'm looking for. I'd give you a good price," Alec said, rubbing the horse's neck.

"She's not for sale," Thomas told him.

Alec looked disappointed but nodded his head in agreement. "If she were mine, I wouldn't sell her either."

Thomas went back to clearing the brambles only to put down the scythe in amazement a few minutes later when Alec led the horse in a walk then a trot around the corral. It had taken him months to get the mare to trust him and follow his lead.

"It seems Mr. Ainsley is rather distracted by your horse," Mattie's voice said beside him.

Thomas turned. Mattie stood in the barnyard, Kathleen balanced on one hip. She was dressed in her Sunday best dress, both sides of her hair pulled back into an elaborate twist. The rest of her hair trailed in gleaming chocolate brown tresses down her back. Thomas swallowed hard and looked down at his boots.

"The man knows his horses," Thomas said.

"He certainly does," Mattie agreed.

"He's going to ruin those good shoes of his," Thomas said petulantly.

Mattie broke out into gales of laughter and clapped Thomas on the arm. Alec turned around at the sound and waved. Smiling, he sauntered back to the barnyard.

"What a horse! Her gait is perfect. And I bet she's fast," he said excitedly. He tipped his hat to Mattie. "Miss Robinson. It's a pleasure. I hope I'm not being too forward when I say that you are looking very lovely this afternoon."

Mattie blushed. "That's very kind of you Mr. Ainsley."

"I hope you'll call me Alec," he said.

"And you must call me Mattie," she told him.

Socks appeared at the top of the ridge barking furiously and running from the direction of the road to Boxwood. They looked up and saw a buckboard approaching, the unmistakable figure of Augustus Hendricks sitting in the driver's seat. Hendricks drove the horses right up to the threesome and stopped short.

"Good day to you, Tom and to your lovely housekeeper," Hendricks said jovially. "And to you, sir," he said to Alec.

"What do you want, Hendricks?" Thomas demanded.

"Is that any way to talk to a neighbor?" Hendricks asked, smiling. His smile widened when he saw the confused look on Thomas' face. "I've just been across the river looking at my new property. Well, it's not mine yet but as soon as I can get a lawyer who's willing to travel this far from civilization I'll claim the two hundred acres across the river from yours."

"Across the river?" Mattie said. "That's John Stark's farm."

"Where he's gone he doesn't need it, does he? Please accept my condolences, ma'am. I heard you were Old Johnny's intended." Hendricks laughed hysterically. "There must be a severe shortage of men in the east if you had to come all the way out here just to marry Johnny Stark."

"Sir, you'd do well to remember your manners," Alec told him sharply, his green eyes flashing.

"Get off my land," Thomas growled. He started toward the buggy.

Hendricks stopped smiling and looked down at him from his perch on the seat of the buckboard. "Fall can't come soon enough. When you default on your loan I'll own farms on both sides of that river." He flicked his wrist and the horses started forward. He turned around in his seat and glared at Thomas. "I'd start packing now if I were you," he called out as he headed down the lane and to the road leading to town.

"He can't just take Mr. Stark's land, can he?" Mattie asked.

"Johnny's gone and he didn't have any kin who might claim the land. All Hendricks has to do is pay a few dollars and farm the land for five years. Then it's all his, free and clear."

"I have a strong feeling that man can't be trusted. Be careful," Alec warned Thomas. "You called him Hendricks. Is that his first name or last?"

"Last. His name is Augustus Hendricks," Thomas said.

Alec furrowed his brow. "That name sounds familiar."

"He came through Boxwood about a year ago. Offered loans to a few of us who had land but no money to get started," Thomas told him.

"No," Alec shook his head. "I feel like I heard that name years ago. Back in Chicago, maybe."

"I thought the name sounded familiar too," Mattie said. "Only I've never been to Chicago. I've never been anywhere but New York City."

Thomas looked out across his fields and toward the river. This was his farm. It wasn't much but it was all he had managed to build in his thirty-six years on earth and Augustus Hendricks would not get his hands on it.

Alec is a perfect gentleman, Mattie thought as she smiled and listened to his story about a horse he owned when he was a boy in Chicago. Dora Bradshaw was right; Alec's passion was horses and he talked endlessly about them. But his stories were funny and engaging and he was charming and likable. He polished off three pieces of the chocolate cake she'd made that morning, a sign that he didn't mind her baking. And he certainly was handsome. He was the perfect combination of sophisticated and sweet. Mattie crossed her ankles and tried not to sigh aloud. So why does he bore me to tears? she asked herself.

CHAPTER ELEVEN

M attie was pacing the length of the porch when Louisa arrived at the farm on Friday afternoon, her little boy Benjamin in tow. She followed the wagon to the barnyard and met her friend with an anxious smile, her hands clasping and unclasping her apron.

"What's wrong?" Louisa asked, reaching up to grab her son and lift him down from the wagon. "You look like you're about to be sick."

"It's silly and it's probably nothing but Thomas didn't come in for the noon meal and I can't see him anywhere in the field. I haven't seen a trace of him since this morning. I'm worrying for nothing. Tell me I'm worrying for nothing," Mattie begged.

Louisa retrieved a basket from the wagon box. "When

was the last time you saw him?"

"At breakfast this morning. This is very unlike him; he's never missed the noon meal...unless he's mad at me. And I don't think he's mad at me although with Thomas it's hard to tell. I had just made up my mind to go looking for him when you drove up," Mattie told her.

"I'll go to the Taylor's ranch and get Alice and Will. Will can go out and look for him," Louisa said.

Mattie shook her head. "No, please don't do that. I'd be completely embarrassed if I was overreacting and Thomas was just busy in the back field and lost track of time." Mattie glanced behind her. "Kathleen's just gone down for her nap. I have about an hour before she wakes up. Would you mind watching her while I go down to the back field and look for Thomas?"

"Of course. Ben and I will find lots to occupy us but I can't promise you they'll be any cookies left by the time you get back," she teased, lifting up the basket.

Grasping her friend's arms in gratitude, Mattie hastily put on her sunbonnet and hurried through the barnyard and into the hayfield. The last time she saw him, Thomas was heading through the hayfield and into the field at the very back of his property. He mentioned something that morning about checking a hole. Or maybe he said he was checking his herd? She groaned in frustration. At the time she was trying to change Kathleen and watch the pancakes so they didn't burn. Why didn't she listen?

At the very back of Thomas' property, the house was only a tiny white speck on the grassland and the river ran rapidly along a bank shaded by short craggy bushes. The loud, high pitched cry of an animal in distress rose above the sound of the rushing water.

"Thomas!" Mattie yelled out. She stalked through the long grass toward the river bank. "Thomas!" Mattie called again.

"Stop yelling, woman! I'm over here," came the reply.

Mattie moved quickly to a copse of trees darkened by the shade. The animal groans intensified. She found Thomas sitting on the ground, his back against the trunk of a cedar tree and his long legs stretched out in front of him.

"Don't call me 'woman'," Mattie told him. She knelt down and peered into the shade. Thomas looked up at her, his face grey and covered with beads of sweat. He gripped his shoulder with his left hand so tightly that the knuckles were white. "What happened?" Mattie asked.

"My shoulder. I think I've pulled my shoulder out of joint," Thomas told her through bared teeth.

Through his shirt, Mattie felt along the top of his shoulder. It was already swollen and the arm hung at an odd angle. "I think you're right. What happened?"

"I was trying to free her," he gestured to a young cow almost hidden in the bushes about ten feet away, her eyes rolling back in her head with fear, bellowing and completely embroiled in a mass of barbed wire. The barbs bit into her flesh with every movement and flies buzzed around the open and bloody wounds.

"The poor girl!" Mattie cried.

"She got scared and knocked me backwards into that tree stump," Thomas explained.

"We have to get her out of here and you back to the house" Mattie told him.

"Hand me those wire cutters." Thomas winced and cried out in pain as he tried to stand up.

"You can't cut wire. You can't even get up." Mattie grabbed the wire cutters and advanced toward the cow. She bellowed and kicked, entangling herself further in the barbed wire. "Stand in front of her and try and keep her still."

"How?" Thomas asked.

"I don't know. I haven't a clue about cows. Are they like horses? Talk gently to her and make little noises," she suggested.

"What kinds of noises?" he said skeptically.

"I don't know, Thomas." Exasperated, she walked toward the cow's neck. *Better to stay away from her legs*, Mattie thought. "Kissing noises."

"I am not making kissing noises," he said flatly.

"Just talk to her. Keep her attention away from me or they'll be two of us with a dislocated shoulder," she said.

While Thomas tried to soothe the animal, Mattie began carefully snipping the wire away from her neck and shoulders. She had to use both hands to bring the blades together to cut the thick wire. By the time she freed the cow's neck and shoulders her hands ached. With her upper body free, the cow was calmer and instead of bellowing and screeching only snorted heavily out of her nostrils. The barbed wire was tightest around her legs. As Mattie snipped away, the barbs dug into and tore jagged scratches on her palms and fingers. Pausing to wipe her bloody hands on her skirt, Mattie suddenly became aware that Thomas was singing. He sang in a deep, clear voice, his Southern drawl more discernible. He caught her watching him.

"The Battle Cry of Freedom," he told her.

Mattie nodded. "I know it. Well, I know the Union version."

"It's the only song I know all the words to. The only song that's fit to sing in front of a lady, that is."

Mattie turned her attention back to the frightened animal and laboriously and steadily removed pieces of barbed wire sections at a time until the cow was free. Tired, she sat down on the grass next to Thomas. "Why in the world would you put barbed wire here?"

Thomas gave her a hard stare. "I didn't but right

across that river is Old Johnny's homestead and Augustus Hendricks was on that land two days ago. I've never believed in coincidences."

"Why would he do this?" Mattie asked.

"To ruin my herd. To get this land," Thomas answered.

"I don't understand why he's so focused on your ranch. There's plenty of land in the Dakota Territory and most of it's being given away for free."

"I don't know but my gut tells me there's a pile more trouble coming this way," Thomas said. He glanced over at the cow. "We've got to get her back to the house and clean out those wounds or we'll lose her."

"Can you walk?" Mattie asked.

"It's my shoulder that hurts, not my legs." Bracing his shoulder with his opposite hand and arm, Thomas struggled to his knees then to his feet. He took two steps and pitched forward. Mattie caught him around the middle and supported his torso with her body.

"It's the pain. Sometimes the pain is so bad it'll make you faint," she told him. "Maybe you should stay here. I can go for help."

Thomas shook his head and breathed in deeply. "That'll take too long."

"Alright then." With one free hand, Mattie reached for Thomas' belt buckle.

He stepped back in shock, his grey eyes wide. "What are you doing, woman?"

"I need to keep your shoulder from moving," she told him. Unbuckling the leather belt, she slid it from the waistband of his pants. Deftly, she wrapped it around his chest and bicep. "This is going to hurt," she warned him. Mattie pulled on the leather and tightened the belt in one hard, swift movement. Thomas moaned. She grasped him around the waist and guided his uninjured arm around her shoulders. "Put all of your weight on me."

"I'll crush you," Thomas protested.

"I'm a big, sturdy girl. I'll be fine," Mattie said.

The walk to the house was agonizingly slow, their footsteps barely a shuffle. Thomas nearly lost consciousness several times but Mattie managed to keep him moving. Finally, they reached the hayfield behind the barn. Mattie's back and arms ached and Thomas' face had gone from ashen to white. She looked toward the house and saw several horses and wagons parked in the barnyard. The door to the house flew open and Louisa tore down the porch steps, through the yard, and into the field.

"What happened? Are you hurt? I've been worried sick!" she called out as she approached. Louisa stopped a moment to catch her breath before noticing Mattie's hands. "You're bleeding!"

"I'm fine. Thomas' shoulder has come out of its socket

and there's an injured cow in the back field by the river," Mattie said.

Three other figures appeared on the porch and, seeing Mattie and Thomas, ran down to meet them. Will and Richard were followed by Alice who held a wailing Kathleen snuggly on her hip, the little girl's face scarlet and her hair sweaty. Mattie enveloped the baby in her arms and Kathleen's screams quieted then faded into ragged breaths.

"You were gone so long and I didn't know what to do. Kathleen woke up from her nap and screamed and screamed for you. I started to get worried so I put the children in the wagon and went to Alice's house. She got Will and we came back here and by that time Richard had arrived wondering where I'd gone," Louisa explained quickly.

"It took us hours to free the cow and walking back was slow," Mattie explained.

"One of your cows was stuck?" Will asked.

"Someone put barbed wire along the river bank," Mattie explained.

"It was Hendricks," Thomas said hoarsely.

"Never mind that," Mattie said. "The cow's wounds need tending to and I need to fix this arm."

"Will, why don't you go and get the cow?" Alice suggested. "That way Richard can take Louisa and Ben home. The poor child is already asleep on the settee."

Will nodded. "I'll bring her up to the barn. You got any salve I can put on her cuts?"

"On a shelf near the horse stalls," Thomas told him.

The women hurried ahead while Richard stayed behind to help Thomas. Once inside, Mattie handed Kathleen to Alice and set about washing her bloodied hands in the wash basin. The baby was finally asleep, breathing heavily with both hands locked into tiny fists. Louisa emerged from the parlor cradling a sleeping Benjamin.

"Thank you for everything. Take that little boy of yours home," Mattie whispered. She squeezed her friend's arm in gratitude.

"I hope you'll join us at the Founder's Day picnic. It's this Sunday," Louisa whispered back.

"I'll try," Mattie promised. Through the open kitchen door she saw Thomas stumbling up the stairs, his hand gripping the railing so hard that his knuckles were white. Sweat rolled down his face and soaked the top of his shirt. Richard stood at the bottom of the stairs and shrugged. Mattie ran to help him but he ignored her and continued up the stairs. "Get to the parlor, you fool," she told him.

Thomas staggered across the kitchen floor to the parlor. Once inside Mattie quietly closed the door and turned to Thomas. "You need to take your shirt off."

With his good hand, he reached for the top button on his shirt but the arm fell wearily to his side. He tried again with the same result.

"It's okay. I can do it," Mattie said, stepping close to him and reaching for the top button on his shirt. Her hands skimmed his chest as she undid the line of buttons to his waist. "I've done this plenty of times before," she said quietly. Realizing how it sounded, she blushed. "I mean I've put an arm back in its socket before." Grasping the front of his shirt, she pulled it slowly from his waistband. Her fingers grazed his stomach and she felt him shudder.

"There's a bottle in the cabinet," Thomas said, his voice ragged.

Mattie nodded and wordlessly turned to the narrow oak cabinet in the corner. Taking out a bottle of whiskey, she popped the cork and handed it to Thomas. He took two swigs and handed it back to her. He raised an eyebrow in surprise when she put the bottle to her lips and took a long sip of the amber liquid. Mattie returned the bottle to the cabinet and began the task of slowly unbuckling the belt binding Thomas' arm to his chest. He moaned as the belt released and the weight of the arm pulled on the socket.

Holding the shirt at the collar, Mattie slid it over Thomas' shoulders and down his arms. Her hand moved along the uneven scars on his left arm, unable to stop herself from touching the rigid muscle underneath his flesh. Thomas breathed in sharply.

"It works best if you lie down." Her voice seemed loud, too loud in the silent room. Thomas held his wounded arm and shoulder with one hand and lowered himself onto the settee. Mattie held his neck and back and guided him until he lay flat, his boots hanging over the end of the short couch. "The pain should ease up once we get the bone back in the socket." She got down on her knees and took his arm, bending it at the elbow. She wrapped a hand around his wrist, braced her knees against the settee and slowly and steadily pulled his arm. Mattie heard a clunk as the bone slid under Thomas' shoulder blade and back into its socket. Clutching his shoulder, Thomas let out a soundless scream.

"Your arm will be weak for a while but I think it should heal nicely," Mattie said, folding one of Kathleen's blankets into a sling. Thomas sat up carefully and she leaned in closely, reaching around his neck to tie the sling.

Thomas looked down at the pink blanket. "How am I supposed to work with this thing on?"

"You're welcome," Mattie said, pointedly.

Thomas reached out and grabbed her arm gently, his eyes looking into hers for the first time since they met. "Thank you."

She shivered at the touch of his rough hands on her skin but made no move to withdraw her arm. Her eyes remained locked with his for several moments until she broke away from his gaze. "I'll bring you a cool cloth for that shoulder to bring the swelling down." Standing up, she crossed the parlor and retreated to the safety of the kitchen, her whole body trembling.

CHAPTER TWELVE

*A*nother day wasted, Thomas thought miserably. *Another damn picnic! A Founder's Day picnic, at that! Boxwood was all of five years old. Why in God's name did they need to celebrate with a picnic?* He kept his eyes straight ahead, desperate to avoid looking at the woman beside him on the wagon seat. The image of her unbuttoning his shirt, the feel of her hands on his chest, the smell of her skin as she leaned in close to him played on a constant loop in his mind for the last few days. Thomas sat up straighter and stretched, hoping to ease the pain in his shoulder. Beside him with Kathleen in her arms, Mattie sighed loudly. She hadn't said a word since they left the ranch but sat silently on the wagon seat, her mouth set in a straight line. She sighed loudly again. Thomas rolled his eyes and cursed under his breath. He knew exactly why she was so sour.

"There's no use pouting over a cake," he told her.

"I'm not pouting!" Mattie snapped. "Children pout. I'm furious." Thomas gave a non-committal grunt. Mattie huffed. "The recipe must have been printed incorrectly or maybe there was something wrong with the eggs. Or the butter. It could have been the butter."

Thomas shook his head. "The butter was fine."

"I really wanted to bring a nice dessert to the picnic," Mattie lamented.

He should be supportive, Thomas decided. Mattie had been close to tears when the cake hadn't turned out. "I'm sure there'll be lots of food. No one will miss your cake."

Mattie stamped her food. "That's not the point, Thomas!" In her arms, Kathleen wiggled and briefly opened her eyes before closing them again. "I tried so hard and followed the recipe exactly. I don't understand why it didn't turn out."

"Maybe you're just not one for cooking," Thomas suggested. This earned him a withering glare. He shifted the reins in his hand and guided the horses around a collection of gopher holes. "Ainsley didn't seem to mind your baking," he added. He couldn't believe that man had been able to shovel three pieces of that dry, tasteless cake into his mouth.

"He was probably just trying to be polite," Mattie said.

Thomas rolled his eyes. "I've never met anybody that polite."

Mattie looked at him, indignant. She tried to hold back

a smile but eventually it broke through. He was amazed at how it lit up her whole face. "I should have left your arm out of its socket."

"I'm mighty glad you didn't," he told her.

Mattie turned toward him. "Why don't you come to the picnic and eat with Kathleen and I? It can't be fun eating all alone in the hotel."

"Eating ain't supposed to be fun," he replied.

"If Mr. Hendricks buys Mr. Stark's land you may want some friends in town," Mattie pointed out.

Why couldn't she see that he didn't want friends? He didn't need friends. He didn't want to go to picnics or get to know his neighbors. He didn't want to be polite and courteous, to talk to people and answer their questions, to curb his bad moods; he just didn't have the energy for it. Thomas expertly guided the horses into a spot in front of the livery. Thomas jumped down from the wagon and offered Mattie his hand to help her down. She looked at him in surprise but took it. He had just handed her the basket of dishes when Mattie saw Will, Alice and Alec walking along the sidewalk across the street. She waved.

"Will you eat lunch with us?" Mattie asked him again.

Thomas shook his head. "I have too many things to do today. I'll meet you back here in two hours." He stalked over to the horses and began unhitching them from the wagon. Mattie crossed the street to meet her friends.

Alec Ainsley rubbed him the wrong way, Thomas admitted to himself. But why? What was it exactly that he had against Ainsley, he wondered. Admittedly, the man was a bit of a dandy and it was wearisome the way he went on and on about horses. But he was genuine and generally affable and could handle horses better than any man he'd ever met. What was it about him that Thomas loathed so much?

Boxwood's founder, Mr. George A. McDougall stood on a small platform in the field behind the general store. The food was laid out on the long tables just as it had been at the spring picnic and Boxwood's settlers milled about. "Folks," McDougall called out. The noise in the crowd gradually died out. "Folks, before we have our meal, I wanted to put forth an idea," he began. "I started thinking last summer that it sure would be nice to have a building, a town hall if you will, where we could come together and hold events like this or discuss matters of importance. A place for funeral services,"

"And weddings!" a young man in the back called out. The crowd laughed.

McDougall chuckled. "And weddings too. I've been mulling this idea over in my head for a while and I've talked with some of our citizens about it. I'm happy to tell you today that Mr. Joshua Ainsley and Mr. Alec Ainsley have graciously offered to donate the wood needed for the building." The crowd clapped and a few men clapped Joshua and Alec on the back and shook their hands.

Alec addressed the crowd. "I donated the wood because anyone who knows me knows I can't build anything. There's quite a few of you here who are still laughing at my attempt to build a chicken coop last spring. We'd need some volunteers to do the carpentry work. I know you're all so busy right now with your fields and on your ranches but this hall would be a real addition to Boxwood. It would be a place to gather with friends and family and not just when the weather's nice outside but all year round. It would be the heart of our community."

"My sons and I will help," Joseph Wilmont said from the crowd.

Beside Alice, Will stood up. "I'll help."

"Me too," Richard Duncan said. His offer was followed by a chorus of voices lending their support and offer of help.

McDougall clapped his hands together joyfully. "This is coming along nicely. Now, we'll also need to raise some money in order to purchase some of the remaining materials such as windows and nails. I know none of us has a lot to spare but I thought we'd pass around a hat and see how much we can collect."

"I don't like that idea," Alice called out. "Not everyone can afford to donate the same amount."

"And it's boring," Louisa added.

"That's exactly what my wife said," McDougall told her. The crowd laughed. "Mrs. Duncan, do you have another idea?"

Louisa shrugged. "I don't have one right now but I'm sure I can think of something. Maybe a dance or something? We could sell tickets."

"I have an idea," Mattie spoke up. She turned around and looked at the crowd. "In case you don't know I'm Mattie Robinson and I arrived here in boxwood about six weeks ago from New York City. In the last few years it has become fashionable to hold boxed lunch socials to raise money."

"Now that sounds like fun. Even though I don't know what it is. Whatever it is, it sounds more entertaining than passing a hat around," Alice said.

"Oh, it's terribly fun," Mattie assured her, excitedly. "Every woman in town makes a lunch for two and puts it in a box or basket that she decorates with pretty ribbons and paper. It's very important that husbands or beaux don't know which basket belongs to which lady. It's supposed to be a secret and it's much more entertaining that way, anyway. All the gentlemen in town get a chance to buy a lunch and eat with the lady who made it. If two gentlemen want the same box they bid for it. It's all in good fun of course and the money would go to the hall."

"That sounds like so much fun! Let's do it!" Clara said happily.

"I have one question." An elderly woman with a cane stood up and addressed Mattie sternly.

"Yes?" Mattie asked.

"Can I do it too?" the woman asked.

Mattie laughed. "Of course."

"I think the women have spoken," McDougall said. "Miss Robinson, since it was your idea would you lead a group of ladies to organize this boxed lunch social?"

Mattie beamed. "I'd love to."

CHAPTER THIRTEEN

Thomas heard his daughter crying from the front porch. Puzzled, he climbed the steps to the door. Since Mattie's arrival, the baby's crying fits had been confined to the middle of the night. He opened the door and entered the kitchen. "How long has the child been like this?" Thomas asked above the din.

Mattie looked up at him from a kitchen chair where she was rocking Kathleen and trying to feed her. "Off and on since she woke up this morning. She won't settle down and I can't get her to eat anything." She carefully wrapped Thomas' uninjured arm around the baby. "I just need a few moments." Exiting the kitchen, Mattie went down the porch steps and headed toward the barnyard. Through the window, Thomas watched her walk from the house to the barnyard for more than ten minutes. Thomas' good shoulder ached but he stayed perfectly still, afraid that if he moved he might drop the child or do something that caused her to cry even louder.

When Mattie returned Kathleen was still crying, her sobs interrupted by the occasional hiccup and yawn.

"She feels awful warm to me. Is a baby supposed to be this warm?" Thomas asked Mattie.

Mattie placed a hand on Kathleen's forehead. "I think you're right. She does feel a little warm. Lay her down in the cradle and I'll try rocking her to sleep again."

Thomas laid her in the cradle and Mattie covered her with a blanket. Kathleen's tired eyes bobbed open and closed while Mattie rocked her.

"Well, why does she feel warm? Has she got a fever? What's wrong with her?" Thomas asked, his questions coming in rapid-fire succession.

"Thomas, I'm sure there's nothing to worry about," Mattie said, gently. "There are about a hundred different reasons why a baby gets a fever. Most of them are nothing to worry about. She could be getting a tooth or she may have the grippe or she may just be feeling poorly today."

"I don't think I could stand more than a few minutes of crying like that," Thomas told her.

"I usually have a great deal of patience but after a few hours of crying I admit that it does wear me down. I've looked after a lot of babies in my time but I've never looked after a child who can cry as loudly or for as long as your Kathleen."

Thomas gave a curt nod. "As long as you don't think there's anything to worry about, then." He stood up and turned to leave.

"I didn't get around to fixing a meal but there is some bread and salt pork if you're hungry," Mattie offered.

"I could eat," Thomas told her.

For once, Mattie was too tired to try and engage him in conversation. They ate their meal in silence, exactly the way Thomas preferred it and when he was finished he nodded, put on his hat and headed back to work.

Late that afternoon Thomas' large boots pounded up the front porch and the front door flew open so fiercely it hit the wall. "Mattie!" he yelled from the kitchen.

Mattie came into the kitchen from the parlor, eyes flashing. "Thomas!" she whispered angrily. "I have spent the last two hours trying to quiet Kathleen!"

Thomas ran up to her and grabbed her arms. "Who did Kathleen play with at the picnic on Sunday?"

"What are you talking about?" Mattie asked.

"At the Founder's Day picnic on Sunday. Who did Kathleen play with? Did she play with any other children?" Thomas demanded. He gripped the tops of her arms harder.

"She's six months old, Thomas. She didn't play with anyone," Mattie answered, shrugging off his hold.

"Was she around any other children?" Thomas thundered.

"Keep your voice down!" Mattie yelled back. "Of course. Ben was there and there was another little girl who was sitting near us at lunchtime," Mattie told him.

"Did you sit near the Johanssons?" Thomas demanded.

"I don't know," Mattie said.

"I need you to think. Did Kathleen play with the little Johansson boy?" Thomas asked.

"I don't think so. I don't know," Mattie told him. "Thomas, what is wrong? What has happened?"

"Will Taylor just rode up when I was in the field. He'd just been to town and heard the little Johansson boy has the measles. So far there are two other families in Boxwood who've come down with it," Thomas explained. He gazed over at the closed parlor door. "Do you think the baby's got it? Is that why she's crying?"

Mattie went pale. "Her fever started getting worse this afternoon. I've been trying to cool her down with cold compresses but it doesn't seem to be working."

"She's so small. She'll never survive this," Thomas yelled. He began pacing back and forth in the kitchen.

Mattie stood up straighter and pulled her shoulders back. "That's enough of that talk," she told him authoritatively. "We don't know anything yet. Kathleen may just have a touch of the influenza or she may be growing fast and just feeling poorly. We don't know right now. We need to keep our wits about us. So far Kathleen only has a fever which could be caused by any number of things. I'll keep a close eye on her for some of the other symptoms. She doesn't have redness of the eyes or a cough yet. I didn't see any spots but I'll go now and have a look."

Thomas followed Mattie into the parlor. Kathleen lay in her crib sleeping fitfully, her few wisps of hair damp and sticking to her skin. Mattie picked her up and she whimpered. "Can you untie her gown?" she asked Thomas. Thomas took the dainty strings of her nightgown in his large hands and untied them. "Do you see any spots on her back?" Mattie asked in a whisper. He shook his head. Mattie turned Kathleen over and removed her nightdress. She breathed a sigh of relief. "Nothing so far." Mattie put Kathleen back in her cradle and covered her with a light blanket.

"She could still have it, though, right? How long does it take to know for sure?" Thomas asked.

"I've seen cases where it's taken almost a week to show any signs,"

"It's only been two days!" he shouted.

Mattie shushed him and led him into the kitchen. "All the more reason to believe this is not the measles." She poured two cups of coffee and placed them on the table. "Kathleen has neither a runny nose or a cough, which usually accompany the high fever." Mattie sat down at the table and took a sip of coffee. She smiled inwardly, proud of herself that she'd finally managed to brew a perfect pot. "I think her fever might just be a coincidence. It seems far too soon for her to be showing any signs of the illness if she was just exposed two days ago."

Thomas sat down across from her and put his head in his hands. "I remember getting the measles. My brother and I both had it. He was nine and I was eight. I remember lying in our bed looking up at the ceiling, sleeping and dreaming and waking up and not being able to tell if I was awake or asleep. And the rash. It felt like fire arts crawling all over my body." He looked up at Mattie. "But we were healthy boys. We could fight it off. The child won't have a chance."

"Quit talking like that," Mattie told him. "There's nothing to do but wait and see."

By supper time Kathleen's fever still hadn't abated. Restless and uncomfortable, she whimpered and cried and wouldn't eat. Thomas and Mattie took turns walking her around the house, inside and outside. They ate at the table while Kathleen wailed in her cradle beside them. Usually, after the evening meal Thomas stood and without much talk left to go back to Johnny's cabin. This time he stood and picked up Kathleen from her cradle.

"I'm not leaving," he told Mattie firmly.

While Thomas held the little girl Mattie wiped her body with a cloth soaked in cool water. She wriggled in his arms and cried more loudly. Mattie and Thomas took turns rocking her and rubbing her back. Finally, she fell into a fitful sleep again.

Mattie sat back on the settee and Thomas collapsed into the chair beside her. "I can't believe you do this every night," he said. "Don't you ever lose patience?"

"Before you start thinking I'm a martyr, I should probably tell you Kathleen's not like this every night. I've got her on a schedule; forty-five minutes of crying and then two, sometimes two and a half hours of sleep. It is taxing but when I feel that I can't take anymore, I put Kathleen down and sit for a few minutes alone outside on the porch. I look around and realize how lucky I am to have ended up here. Then I come inside and start all over again."

"You're a good woman," Thomas said. He blushed and cleared his throat. "I mean you're capable. Level headed. A real hard worker."

Mattie smiled ruefully. It stung just a bit being praised for such mundane qualities. *A hard worker?* she thought. *Level headed and capable? I sound like an old plow horse or a hunting dog.* She curled up and tucked her feet under her. "I didn't know you had a brother. Is he back east?"

"He was killed somewhere in Virginia," Thomas answered.

"I'm so sorry," Mattie said. "What about your parents?"

"My father died while I was in the prison camp; my ma followed him about two months after I came back home," Thomas said, his eyes closed.

"And Susannah?" she asked hesitantly. "I mean, did you marry her before the war?"

"No. After," he answered. His curt reply and unwillingness to offer any details told Mattie that the subject was closed.

"I envy you," Mattie said. Thomas looked at her quizzically. "I don't mean I envy that you lost your wife! My goodness, no! I'm envious of anyone who got a chance to know their family. Even if all you have now are memories it's more than I have. All I know about my mother is that she was poor, unmarried and with child, like so many of the women Dr. Preston tends to. Oh, I'm not complaining," Mattie said quickly. "I was very lucky to end up with Dr. and Mrs. Preston. They are wonderful, caring people and they took me in and raised me like I was their own daughter. I know you think it was very foolish of me to come all the way out here from New York City to marry a man I didn't know but I had hoped so desperately that Mr. Stark... Well, I had hoped to have a family of my own."

"I imagine you'll get the chance," Thomas said.

"I hope so," Mattie told him.

The time crawled and Kathleen woke up every hour crying. Mattie checked her thoroughly for spots but found none. Thomas rocked her and walked her up and down the length of the kitchen, at first holding her stiffly but then gradually relaxing. When his arms got tired Mattie took over. During the short periods where Kathleen slept, the two sat in companionable silence, neither concerned with making small talk, both of them too tired to feel ill at ease with one another. They fell in and out of consciousness, until Mattie woke with a start and glanced at the clock on the mantel. Kathleen had been asleep for almost three hours. *Kathleen never sleeps for three hours*, Mattie thought, panic rising from her chest to her throat. She jumped up from the settee and raced over to the cradle. Kathleen's little chest moved up and down, her hair still damp with sweat but her cheeks no longer flushed. Mattie felt her forehead. No sign of fever.

"Thomas!" she called quietly. He was dozing in the chair and shook his head, startled. "She's fine. Kathleen's fine." Mattie said excitedly.

"She's alright?" Thomas stood.

"Her fever's gone. She's sleeping peacefully," she said.

Thomas peeked into the cradle and a smile spread across his face. "She's alright." He turned to Mattie and his expression once more took on a worried countenance. "Is she in the clear? It can't be the measles?"

"I don't think so. Mind you, I haven't had much experience dealing with the measles but from what I understand if she had the measles her fever wouldn't have broken. I'll check her for spots when she wakes up and I'll look inside her mouth too to see if I can see any little white sores but I think she's fine. It must have been something else that caused the fever."

"She's okay. She's going to be okay," he repeated.

Sighing heavily, Thomas rested his forearm gently on Mattie's shoulder, put his head down on his arm and took a deep breath. Mattie reached up and patted his shoulder soothingly. He looked up slowly, the hard stubble of his beard brushing against her cheek. She shivered at the unfamiliar sensation. She looked at him boldly and his grey eyes darkened. They both leaned in slowly, hesitantly. His lips touched hers softly and gently at first but when she eagerly returned the kiss it became hard and devouring. She slid her hands up his back, trailing her long fingers up his neck and into his hair. He clutched her around the waist and pulled her closer to him. Mattie gasped loudly at the feel of his hard chest against the rounded softness of her body. Thomas opened his eyes and backed away, his breath ragged.

"I apologize. I'm sorry. That was completely improper of me. I don't know what I was thinking," he mumbled, looking away from her.

Mattie felt the heat of a blush staining her face. "You were happy, that's all. I take no offense."

"It didn't mean anything. I don't think of you..in that way," Thomas explained.

Humiliation and disappointment wound themselves tightly around her heart. Mattie forced a smile. "And I don't think of you that way either."

"Now that I know the baby's fine I'll be heading back to Johnny's cabin," Thomas said. He stalked out of the parlor. Mattie heard the front door open then slam shut and the sound of his heavy boots fade away as he walked off the porch and away from the house.

Mattie looked down at the sleeping child in the cradle, realizing too late that she'd set herself up for heartache. She loved this little girl so much, as if she were her own and she was starting to feel the same about Thomas. Only Thomas wasn't hers. He didn't want a wife; he needed a nanny and a cook. He didn't want to add to his family; Kathleen was enough. She could have accepted all of these things bravely but it was his assertion that he didn't even see her as a woman that broke her.

Chapter Fourteen

Sitting alone on the porch, Mattie tried to decide if she was angry or relieved Alec hadn't shown up as promised to court her that afternoon. She poured herself another cup of lukewarm tea and gave one of her freshly baked biscuits to Socks. She should feel incensed that he left her waiting in her best dress, hair done and tea prepared but, if she was perfectly honest with herself, she wasn't even disappointed. She wasn't sure she could endure another conversation about horses and he looked bored every time she mentioned New York City and her experiences working alongside Dr. Preston, nor did he seem to have any interest in Kathleen. Their conversations were polite but uninteresting.

She was still pondering what to do about Alec when he arrived more than an hour late, his team galloping at full speed into the yard. After tending quickly to his team, he took off his hat and waved to her excitedly. "Please forgive me for being late but the most extraordinary thing has happened," he called even before he reached the porch.

"Of course," Mattie said. "I hope nothing is wrong."

"Not at all. Everything is finally working out!" Alec's eyes danced. He waited for Mattie to sit down and then took the chair beside her. "Nearly four years ago I met a man who had a horse ranch in Mexico. He'd been working the better part of twenty years to build up his herd and he managed to breed the most beautiful horses I have ever seen. I wanted to buy several to start my own operation up here but he wouldn't part with any of them. I was disappointed but I liked the old guy and I stayed in Mexico for a bit. He taught me more about horses than I thought possible. Over the years I kept in touch, sending letters in my terrible Spanish which greatly delighted him according to his son. This morning I received a telegram saying that he was ready to part with twenty horses of my choosing and I should come to Mexico immediately." He popped up out of his chair. "This is what I wanted all along. I wanted to build the best horse farm in the territory. Now I've finally got the chance." He looked down at his cotton shirt and heavy work pants. "I didn't even have time to change before coming here. I've been sending telegrams and gathering supplies all morning."

"How wonderful, Alec! When do you leave?" Mattie asked.

"Tomorrow at first light," he answered.

"That's quick," Mattie said. "How long will you be gone?"

"A few months, I think," he said. He sat back down and took his hat in his hands, his expression serious. "I need to be honest with you, Mattie. I'm not sure when I'll be back to Boxwood. It could be months and even when I get back I want to focus on my herd and build my reputation in the horse business. I want to make money," he laughed. "I'm just saying I don't think you should wait around for me."

Mattie patted his hand. Unlike when she touched Thomas, no shivers ran up and down her back. "You're a gentleman to the core, Alec Ainsley. And you're handsome and smart and ambitious and kind but I suspect neither you nor I have any intention of waiting on each other."

Alec smiled sheepishly. "I guess there's no harm in admitting we're not suited to one another."

"No there isn't. I hope when you return you'll stop by and share a few tales of your adventures," Mattie said.

"I will." Alec walked halfway down the steps turned back around. "I didn't have a chance anyway, really."

"What do you mean?" Mattie asked, perplexed.

Alec looked out into the field where Thomas was tending to his cows. "Someone else already caught your interest.

I knew the first time I saw you looking at him." He set his hat on his head and grinned rakishly. "Take care Mattie."

Mattie watched him disappear into the unending expanse of field and sky and wondered just how much longer she could keep her growing feelings a secret from Thomas.

Alice picked Mattie up in the buckboard the following afternoon to meet with the four other ladies on the Boxed Social Committee and finalize the details of the event. Once they arrived at the livery in town, Mattie descended from the wagon, Kathleen sleeping peacefully in her sling.

"Would you mind terribly if I ran to see Dora Bradshaw for a few moments?" Mattie asked her friend.

Alice narrowed her eyes. "Not at all. I'll tell the other ladies you'll be a few minutes but you need to tell me what's wrong."

"What do you mean?" Mattie asked.

"You hardly said four words all the way into town," Alice said.

Mattie smiled. "I guess I'm tired. Kathleen is much better during the day now but she still cries for several hours at night. It's draining."

Alice nodded sympathetically. "How silly of me. I didn't think of that. You run along and find Dora and I'll tell the other ladies you'll be a few minutes."

"Thank you." Mattie squeezed her friend's hand and started off toward the Bradshaw house at the end of the street.

Dora was home hanging a basket of wet laundry on the line. She finished hanging up a sheet and then boldly hugged Mattie. "I was hoping you'd come by for a visit," Dora said. Her smile faded when she looked closely at Mattie's face. "But why do I think this isn't such a happy occasion?"

"I've come by to ask for your help," Mattie said.

"Of course, dear." Dora led her to two chairs outside of the kitchen door and sat down. "What is it?"

"I was hoping that you could write to some of your friends or relatives and help me locate a position. Perhaps as a governess. Or a lady's companion," Mattie asked.

"What did that man do this time?" Dora asked, exasperated.

"Nothing," Mattie said. Seeing Dora's skeptical expression, she reassured her. "Thomas has done nothing. He is as he has always been. And now that Kathleen has settled a great deal it seems a good idea to move on."

"Very interesting," Dora said. "I wasn't talking about Thomas. I was talking about Alec."

"Alec is leaving for Mexico tomorrow morning to bring back a herd of Spanish horses. We have decided that we weren't particularly well suited," Mattie told her.

"I believe that but I don't believe this malarky about Thomas," Dora said.

"Thomas has made it very clear that likes his life the way it is. My part in his life is temporary," Mattie said.

"Now I understand," Dora nodded.

"I need to leave. Before I let my imagination run wild and start imagining things that could never be," Mattie told her.

"I don't think it's just your imagination you're afraid of running wild. I think you're afraid your heart will run wild too," Dora said gently. Mattie nodded and began to cry. "Buck up, dear," Dora patted her on the back. "If you're serious about leaving I have a few friends in Chicago and a cousin in Saint Louis. I'll write to them today but it may take several months. You of all people know how slow the mail is."

Mattie dried her eyes and squared her shoulders. "Thank you, Dora. You're a good friend. I must be heading back to the hotel. Alice and the ladies on the boxed social committee are waiting for me."

"Are you sure there isn't any way you can fix this?" Dora asked.

Mattie shook her head sadly. "I think it's time to move on."

CHAPTER FIFTEEN

M attie did her best to avoid Thomas for the next week and it seemed like he was doing his part to avoid her too. He entered brusquely for the noon meal and, muttering about falling behind in his work, he grabbed some cheese and bread and quickly left again, stomping back out to the field. At suppertime Mattie busied herself with Kathleen, fussing with her and tending to imaginary tasks that took her to the parlor or required her to stand at the stove, her back to Thomas.

The first Saturday morning in June dawned unusually hot and close and by early morning the heat had grown so oppressive and heavy that Mattie found it difficult to breathe and had to loosen the laces on her corset. Kathleen squirmed and whined, uncomfortable and cranky. Shortly before noon Thomas sat down on the front porch and sighed. His shirt was soaked with sweat and his face was red.

He noticed Mattie standing in the doorway. "Unusual weather," he remarked, swiping his wet hair back from his face. An awkward silence stretched between them. "It was cooler down by the river. We could all go and escape this heat. If you wanted to."

Mattie brightened. "I'll make us a picnic."

The group of three set off a few minutes later. Mattie carried the basket of food in the crook of her elbow, a folded blanket laid on top. Thomas held Kathleen in one arm, easily and gently and Mattie marveled at how comfortable he had become holding his daughter. Every so often he leaned into Kathleen's neck and she giggled in delight and patted his face. As they approached the riverbank, Mattie felt the air get cooler and a light breeze blew between the tall grass. Thomas led them to a level spot under an oak tree and taking the blanket, shook it out and laid it on the grass. He set Kathleen down on her back and she quickly rolled over onto her stomach. Her legs kicked and she dug her elbows into the ground. She moved forward slightly.

"Did you see that? She moved!" Thomas said excitedly.

Mattie couldn't help but laugh. "She figured that out this morning quite by accident. Her doll was just out of her reach and she desperately wanted it. She kicked and reached and pretty soon she moved herself forward ever so slightly. You should have seen the look on her face. She seemed completely amazed."

Their eyes held each other's gaze for a moment too long and Mattie felt a flush of heat in her face. She looked away and busied herself unpacking the food. Thomas looked away too and watched Kathleen.

"I need to apologize," he said finally. "I've made things awkward between us. It wasn't right for me to kiss you. I just got caught up and ...Well, I apologize."

"You have nothing to apologize for. I should never have kissed you back. I forgot myself for a moment. It won't happen again."

"Absolutely not," Thomas agreed.

"Well then, now everything can go back to the way it was," Mattie said brightly. She swallowed the hard lump in her throat.

"Sure," Thomas agreed.

Mattie reached over and helped Kathleen roll back onto her back. The little girl grasped her little doll and moved it from hand to hand, occasionally bringing it up to her mouth to chew on it.

"I miss the beach at Coney Island," Mattie said suddenly, looking out across the river. "I can truly say that it's the only thing I miss about New York. Every summer I'd try and find the most perfect day and take the ferry. Dr. Preston was always worried about me so he'd unearth some terrible suitor to go with me. Most of the time they'd end up abandoning me but I didn't care. I'd go for the whole day. I just wanted to feel the sand and see the ocean."

"I saw the ocean once when I was marching through Charleston. Didn't care for it," Thomas said.

Mattie shook her head and laughed. "Thomas Langley! Only you would find fault with something as beautiful as the ocean."

"I miss our bathing hole," Thomas said, staring at the river. "On really hot days, my brother Tobias and I would wait until we were sure Father wouldn't catch us neglecting our chores and we would run down to the bathing hole. There was a tree that had fallen just so that we could climb it and jump off into the water."

"That sounds lovely," Mattie said.

"It was. Of course, at the time, all I could think about was getting far away from home. There never seemed to be enough action for my liking and my father and I were always butting heads. Like most young men I didn't like being told what to do," he said.

"Is that why you left to fight in the war?" Mattie asked carefully.

"I fought in the war because that's what was expected," Thomas answered. "Though, I guess in the beginning I looked upon it as a big adventure. We all did. 'Til the killing started."

"I won't pretend to know what that feels like," she told him. "I saw a lot of young men return badly wounded, some missing arms and legs and some no longer right in the head. It was a lot to bear for many families."

"My ma didn't know I had survived until I showed up at the farm two months after the war ended. Only by then it wasn't our farm anymore. All the farms in the county had been taken over by carpetbaggers. I found Ma living in a tarpaper shack on the edge of the property with Susannah."

"Your wife?" Mattie asked.

Thomas nodded. "Her father owned the farm next to ours. She was just an annoying little kid when I left, always getting in our way and trailing after Tobias like a puppy. By then her parents and all four of her brothers were gone. After my ma passed on I decided to make my way out here and Susannah…" he stopped, struggling to find the right words.

"Came along too?" Mattie suggested.

"We got married," Thomas said, indignantly. "It was all proper and legal."

"I wasn't implying otherwise," she said quickly.

"Susannah had a real hard time with everything. She lost her parents, her brothers and her home. Then I dragged her out here without a damn care for what she wanted. She lost Matthew. I wasn't easy to live with and I sure wasn't easy to talk to. The truth is, I wasn't a good husband. I didn't even try. Susannah deserved better," Thomas said.

"She probably did," Mattie agreed. "But life only moves in one direction and that's forward. The only thing you can do about it now is to be a good father to Kathleen and make sure she knows how much her mother loved her, how much you love her. It also wouldn't hurt to be less surly. The war is over Thomas; it's been over for two years. You need to put it to rest. We're all out here because we want a fresh start. So make a fresh start."

"You're one to talk about starting fresh," Thomas said, angrily.

"And just what do you mean by that?" Mattie frowned.

He shrugged and looked away but he couldn't escape her persistent stare. "You still think of yourself as the ugly old spinster who had to become a mail order bride to find herself a husband."

Mattie's eyes flashed and she clamped her lips together. "I do not."

"You're always making comments about your looks," Thomas pointed out.

"Oh, for pity's sake!" Mattie waved her hand in the air. Avoiding his gaze, she busied herself straightening and arranging Kathleen's dress. "I'm realistic, Thomas. I'm not a great beauty. Men have never fallen all over themselves to court me nor are they ever likely to. I'm not demure or dainty or soft spoken. I don't giggle or pretend I'm helpless. I'm opinionated and I talk too much. I don't like being told what to do. I'm a big girl used to hard work and I'm proud that I can deliver a baby and stitch up a bad cut. None of these qualities are ones that men look for in a woman. They're not, as I've been reminded many times by countless women who thought they were being helpful, valuable traits in a wife."

Thomas snorted and Mattie crossed her arms and glared at him haughtily. "I suppose you don't think women should talk about such things."

"I was just thinking that was the stupidest thing I've ever heard," Thomas answered.

"I beg your pardon!" she yelled.

"Mattie, think about it. It makes no sense. Your lady friends are telling you that every man likes the same type of woman. That just can't be. Dora Bradshaw and Alice Taylor are two entirely different women and their husbands like them just fine," he pointed out. "It seems to me that all of those qualities you see in yourself as disagreeable are ones you should be damn proud of. They're ones a woman needs to survive, married or not. Especially out here. But hell, what do I know?" Thomas finished lamely.

Mattie bit her lip and looked out at the river. She watched the fast-moving current carry a thick branch downstream, smashing it against rocks and dragging it underwater along the way. She smiled slowly. "I guess this place really isn't for the demure and dainty."

"Wait 'til winter," Thomas muttered.

They sat in silence for a few minutes, content to watch Kathleen flip onto her stomach and inch herself forward, gurgling and kicking her legs happily.

Thomas finally spoke up. "What exactly is in that food basket, woman?"

"Don't call me woman," Mattie told him. "Or I won't share any of it with you."

"I might be better off hungry," Thomas smiled slightly.

"I'll have you know that I have learned to make wonderful bread these last six weeks. It's almost perfect," Mattie said.

"I don't think I'd go that far," Thomas snorted.

When the sun dipped low in the sky, Thomas collected the basket and blanket and Mattie picked up Kathleen who was breathing deeply and on the verge of sleep. They walked back up the path and Mattie paused to look back at the river. On the other side of the bank she saw the roof of a small building.

"Is that Mr. Stark's land over there?" she inquired.

Thomas nodded. "The river divides our farms."

"Is the house far from here?" she asked. "I can only see that small barn."

"That's the house," he informed her. "Old Johnny never saw the need for much. He was content with a roof over his head and a fire to keep himself warm. Would you like to see it?" Thomas asked impulsively. He didn't want to think too deeply about his reasons for offering to show her Johnny's place. If he thought too hard about it, examined it too closely he was afraid he'd have to admit that it had nothing to do with avoiding work and everything to do with prolonging his time with Mattie and he couldn't let his mind wander in that direction. "Had circumstances been different you'd be living there right now."

Mattie smiled. "I suppose you're right. Let's walk a while and take a look."

Thomas finished walking up the steep river bank. "Johnny started making a culvert a ways down the field. It's high and dry and the perfect place to cross onto his place."

They walked through the field, crossing the culvert and approaching the farmhouse from the back.

The house was hardly larger than the chicken coop at Thomas' farm. The roof sagged in the middle but the weathered boards on the walls were sturdy. The broken panes of glass in the lean-to's only window were patched with oilcloth and the only door hung slightly askew. Thomas reached out to pull the leather strap that served as a knob and the door opened, rubbing roughly against the ground. Mattie entered and stood for a moment, taking in the old wood stove, the dirt floor and the few pieces of old furniture. Thomas tried to imagine her living in the lean-to with Johnny but couldn't. She didn't fit. Somehow he could only see her in his house, cooking dinner on his stove, walking up and down the stairs with his child, touching him in his parlor. He turned and his gaze fell on the wardrobe in the corner, its door slightly ajar. Crossing the room in three strides, he wrenched the wooden door open. "Someone's been in here," he said.

"How can you tell?" Mattie asked, going to him.

"This wardrobe was locked when Johnny died and I never opened it. I don't have the key." Thomas examined the locked. "It's broken."

"Why would anyone break into a wardrobe?" Mattie asked.

"I don't know. It must have happened when I was out in the field this morning," Thomas said.

Mattie peered inside. "It's just papers." She touched a leather-bound book. "The family Bible. Hardly anything worth stealing."

Thomas looked thoughtfully into the wardrobe. "Unless papers were exactly what they were looking for." Mattie looked at him, confused. "I don't know for sure, but I'm pretty sure this is where Johnny kept the deed to his farm. He also had an old survey of these parts too."

Mattie reached into the wardrobe and searched through a box of papers. "No survey. And I don't see a deed either." She stopped unexpectedly at a vanilla colored envelope and smiled sadly. "My letter," she said.

"He read that letter over and over," Thomas said. "He was mighty excited that you were coming."

"Even though you told him he was an old fool and it was a terrible idea?" Mattie teased. She searched throughout the wardrobe. "There's nothing here, Thomas. It's just my letter and some paperwork from the army. Here's a recipe for syrup to stop coughs." Mattie held up a piece of paper and skimmed it. "Oh my goodness. I hope Mr. Stark didn't actually use this. Coal oil is one of the ingredients."

"Hendricks," Thomas said. "It has to be Hendricks."

CHAPTER SIXTEEN

T homas guided the wagon into the livery early Monday morning with the intention of visiting Sheriff Bradshaw and informing him about the events of the previous week.

"I promised to meet Alice, Clara and Louisa at the hotel for tea," Mattie reminded Thomas, passing Kathleen to him carefully before climbing down from the wagon.

"So you said." His shoulder was still weaker than usual but he'd stopped using the sling and it could bear a small amount of weight. Thomas cradled his daughter carefully and patted her head affectionately before handing her back to Mattie.

"Will you join us?" Mattie asked.

"Tea with a bunch of ladies? I don't think so," Thomas replied.

"Suit yourself," Mattie sighed.

They strolled along the sidewalk together and when Mattie stopped at the general store to examine several new dresses in the window, Thomas leaned against the store-front and watched Boxwood's residents go about their morning routines. Suddenly, Mattie felt him tense beside her. He stood up to his full height and crossed his arms. She looked to the left and saw Augustus Hendricks scurrying down the sidewalk in their direction.

Hendricks touched the brim of his hat to Mattie. "Good day to you, miss."

"Mr. Hendricks." She stared at him coldly.

Thomas took a large step closer to him, hands clenched. "You're a thief!"

"I beg your pardon, Mr. Langley. What are you talking about?" Hendricks asked, laughing.

"You went into Mr. Stark's house, broke into the wardrobe and stole the deed to his land and a map," Mattie said.

"Ridiculous!" Hendricks told her. "What an imagination you have, Miss Robinson."

"The lock was forced open and somebody rifled through all of Johnny's important papers. The map and the deed are gone," Thomas said.

"That is truly terrible. Nothing is safe anymore. This territory is full of thieves and outlaws," Hendricks replied.

"It was you!" Thomas shouted.

"You are mistaken," Hendricks said. "Why would I need to steal a deed and a map when I plan to buy the land anyway? Just as soon as a lawyer passes through to certify and register the sale the farm will be mine. You might want to start looking around for alternative sleeping arrangements, Tom. If that is still a concern." He smiled suggestively.

"You're a horrible man," Mattie told him.

Throwing his head back, Hendricks laughed heartily. "Oh my dear, I've been called worse by the sisters at Our Lady of the Assumption." Touching the brim of his hat, Hendricks walked around them and continued down the street.

Thomas looked over at Mattie. Her face was pensive. "There's nothing to worry about. I'll talk to the Sheriff."

Mattie shook her head. "It's not that. Remember when I said before that the name Augustus Hendricks sounded familiar? Now I feel as if Our Lady of the Assumption sounds familiar too."

"There's bound to be a church called Our Lady of the Assumption in New York," Thomas said.

"Possibly. But no," Mattie thought for a few seconds. "No, I feel like I've heard the name Augustus Hendricks associated with the church Our Lady of the Assumption. And something tells me it wasn't anything good." Mattie said.

Mattie glanced over at the telegraph office and caught Joshua locking the door. "Joshua!" she called out.

The young man turned around and smiled. "Mattie. How are you this morning?"

"I'm just fine," she paused. "Or rather, I'm not. I don't know."

"What's wrong?" Joshua asked, concerned.

"I saw that you were just locking up but I was wondering if I could possibly send a message? It's very important," Mattie said.

"Of course. I was just heading out to do some errands. I hope everything's alright," he said, opening the door. Mattie followed him into the narrow office, Thomas right behind her. Joshua reached for a piece of paper and a pencil. "Where's this telegram going?"

"Rose Bennett, Fifth Avenue, Manhattan, New York," Mattie told him.

Joshua whistled. "That's quite the address."

"What are you doing?" Thomas asked.

"The name Augustus Hendricks seems too familiar. So does Our Lady of the Assumption. Rose is a good friend and if there's something to know about either of those two names she'll know it. Or find out for me," Mattie explained.

"What do you want me to write?" Joshua asked.

"Tell her I'm looking for information about Augustus Hendricks or Our Lady of the Assumption and to contact me immediately," Mattie instructed.

"I'll send this out right now," Joshua promised. "You know, my brother mentioned the name sounded familiar to him too."

Thanking him again, Mattie and Thomas stepped out of the telegraph office and walked slowly toward the general store.

"What do you think Hendricks is involved in?" Thomas asked.

"I wish I could remember," Mattie said. "I just know I've heard that name before." Mattie pushed aside her thoughts of Augustus Hendricks. "You're sure you won't join Kathleen and I?"

"I'll eat by myself when I'm done talking to the Sheriff. Don't concern yourself with me," he replied.

Mattie nodded her head and set Kathleen on her hip. After parting ways with Thomas in front of the hotel, Mattie entered its doors and made her way through the lobby and into the dining room. The room was crowded and noisy but she spotted Alice waving from a table near the back.

"Thank goodness you were here before me to get a table," Mattie said, walking up to her friends.

Louisa poured her a cup of tea. "It's the fifteenth of the month. Mrs. Millburn cooks up a Scottish dinner on the fifteenth of every month. It's quite popular."

Once Mattie had her cup of tea in hand and had selected a biscuit from a bowl in the middle of the table, Clara wasted no time in bringing up the subject of Alec's departure.

"It is such a pity that Alec had to go off to Mexico," she said to Mattie.

"This is quite an opportunity for him," Mattie said. "I'm glad he'll have the chance to build up his own herd. He seems very excited."

"Perhaps when he returns…" Clara started.

"I don't think so," Mattie told her. She leaned in closer to Clara. "Alec is lovely but I think we're destined to just be good friends."

"How disappointing!" Clara pouted. She paused. "You know, Joshua has a cousin…"

"Clara," Louisa warned. "Are you playing matchmaker?"

"Well, Harold wrote in his last letter that he was starting to feel that it was time to find a wife and settle down."

Alice made a face. "Harry? You're thinking of unleashing Harry on poor Mattie? Ugh."

Mattie looked at Clara. "What's wrong with Harry?"

"I suppose there's nothing wrong with him. He's just incredibly boring and dull but maybe he would be more talkative and interesting if he met you," Clara suggested.

"Well, at least he's not ill-natured," Alice said. She pointed to the hotel's front door. "Isn't that Mr. Langley standing all by himself over there?"

Mattie turned and looked. "It is," she said, puzzled. She handed Kathleen to Alice. Kathleen whined and squirmed, arms outstretched. Mattie kissed her on the nose. "I wonder if something is wrong." She got up and skirted the crowded little tables until she reached Thomas. "I thought you were going to talk to the Sheriff," she said.

"He's out until this afternoon. Dora's going to give him my message," he said.

"Why don't you join us?" Mattie asked.

Thomas hesitated and looked around. "I'm used to eating by myself."

"There isn't much chance of that happening today," Mattie gestured to the crowded dining room. "Mrs. Millburn's cock-a-leekie soup is clearly a favorite. You might have to wait an hour or more for a table all by yourself. "

He sighed. "I'll join you then."

Mattie smiled. "Don't look so happy, Thomas," she said, as she led him back to the table. He pulled out the extra chair and sat down, dwarfing everyone. Without asking, Mattie poured tea into a dainty china cup and handed it to him. He scowled at it but took a drink, reaching for a biscuit from the bowl at the same time. She passed him the dish of butter and a clean knife.

"Nice to see you, Mr. Langley," Alice said.

"And you," Thomas mumbled back.

"How is the progress on the new community building, Alice?" Mattie said, breaking the silence and changing the subject.

"It's going well. Will said the walls are up and Joseph Wilmont and his sons say they'll get the roof up this week. It will be so nice to have a place to gather in town," Alice said.

"It'll be pretty basic, I'm afraid," Louisa said. "Most of the men in this town can build a barn but they're not too handy at building anything fancier than that."

Mattie perked up. "Thomas could help," she offered. Thomas stopped chewing mid-mouthful and stared at her. "You know that porch on his house? Thomas carved all of those spindles and did all of the decorative trim," Mattie told them.

"That porch is beautiful," Louisa said.

"A little bit of trim at the front would pretty it up a bit. Maybe around the door?" Alice said.

"It's too bad that we couldn't have a stage made for the inside with a podium," Clara mused. "So the children could but on pageants or present their work."

"We could!" Mattie said excitedly. "Thomas can do all of that. His work is beautiful."

"No!" Thomas thundered.

Alice, Louisa and Clara shrank back. Mattie set her teacup firmly on its saucer. "Why not?"

"I don't have time to build stages and carve trim. I have a ranch to run," Thomas sneered.

"Perhaps we should discuss this later," Mattie suggested.

In reply, Thomas stood up, shoved his hat on his head and stalked out of the dining room and the hotel lobby.

Alice let out a deep breath. "Honestly, Mattie, I don't know how you put up with that man. He's frightening."

Mattie had to agree. It seemed that Thomas had listened to her suggestion about controlling his ornery behavior but had decided not to act upon it.

The atmosphere in the wagon on the ride home was glacial. When she could stand it no longer, Mattie stared Thomas down. "You didn't have to be so rude," she began.

He returned her stare, his face heated. "You didn't have any right to offer my help," he roared.

Mattie refused to back down. "And you could have politely refused instead of stalking off like a..." Mattie paused. "like a child. That's right! You stomped off like a petulant child who had just been refused a second piece of cake."

"You should mind your own business!" Thomas yelled.

"This town is my business!" she yelled back. "I think your carpentry work is beautiful and that you're incredibly talented. I thought you would want to share that with the town, contribute and be part of Boxwood."

"I don't want to be a part of anything. I just want to live on my farm and be left alone," Thomas grumbled.

"No man can exist completely alone. It's impossible!" Mattie raised her voice. "It's not natural either. We are supposed to be a part of a community, to help each other and to share in each other's joys and sorrows."

"I've had enough sorrow to last a lifetime," Thomas muttered.

"Then maybe it's time for some joy," Mattie countered.

CHAPTER SEVENTEEN

When Thomas climbed the stairs to the front door on Wednesday he could smell the scent of frying pork chops and freshly baked bread. He looked over at the clean laundry hanging on the line rippling slightly in the breeze and at the neatly tended garden. How long had it been since he looked forward to entering his own house? Had he ever felt like this? Guilt gripped him, deep and low in his belly.

Mattie turned and smiled at him when he entered. "Yes, that is bread that you smell and I'm quite confident that this time it will be delicious. Alice gave me a hand."

Thomas took off his hat and placed it on the table. He walked over to the stove and poured himself a cup of coffee. "I thought I saw the Taylor's wagon up here."

"Yes. Poor Alice. She was furious with Will this morning," Mattie told him. "He wouldn't listen to Alice at all. He was being completely unreasonable and Alice was in tears."

Thomas sat down and took a sip of the coffee. Better than the day before; hardly any grounds made it into the coffee this time. "Marriage is hard," he told Mattie.

"Alice volunteered to do some painting in the new community building this Saturday and Will pitched a fit and forbade her. He said it was too dangerous in her condition and that he wanted her to stick close to home for the next few months. Alice was beside herself," Mattie said.

"Will's right," Thomas said.

Mattie stopped stirring the pot of beans and glared at him. "Not you too?"

"A woman in Alice's delicate condition should be at home resting and doing quiet things like sewing or needlework. She should be where her husband can find her in case something happens, not climbing ladders to paint walls and certainly not driving a buckboard around by herself all over the countryside," Thomas told her.

"Alice is having a baby; she's not on her deathbed. Women have been having babies since the beginning of time. And doing laundry and tending chickens and cooking meals and doing the hundreds of other things a woman does in a day. Besides, she has a few months yet before she needs to stick closer to home," Mattie said.

"Too many things can go wrong with a baby. She should listen to her husband," Thomas declared loudly.

"And she will. For now, anyway. But that doesn't mean she has to like it," Mattie told him, her voice equally as loud. "Since Alice can't do the painting in the hall she came to ask me if I could do it. I told her I'd be happy to help out. Evan Wilmont can drive me into town on Saturday if you're too busy. I'll take Kathleen, of course."

"Evan Wilmont?" Thomas said.

"Joseph Wilmont's oldest son," Mattie said. "He's such a nice man. He's been working on the hall with Will. He was at the Taylors' this morning and when he heard Alice couldn't do any painting, he suggested she ask me. Then he kindly offered to come by and pick me up since it's on his way and he was planning to do some work at the hall on Saturday anyway."

On his way? He lives ten miles out on the other side of Boxwood! Thomas thought. This was just an attempt to get Mattie alone. He didn't trust the man. Thomas set his coffee cup down.

"I have to go to the store on Saturday to buy some supplies. I can take you," he told her.

Mattie brightened. "Wonderful! Will Taylor is stopping by later today and I'll let him know. I'm so glad I won't have to bother Mr. Wilmont."

Thomas smirked into his coffee cup. He was sure Evan Wilmont wouldn't have found it a bother.

On Saturday morning Thomas pulled the buckboard up to the hall instead of the livery. The new building sat on a lot at the end of town in a field full of wild prairie flowers, its walls of freshly sawn logs and its roof a bright red tin. The windows had yet to be installed but the double door stood in place, large and welcoming. It was sturdy and proud, serviceable and unadorned, much like the residents of Boxwood themselves. Carrying Kathleen on her hip, Mattie climbed the stairs and pushed open the doors. The inside was empty except for a raised platform at the front of the room that would serve as a stage.

"There are still benches to make but I think it's wonderful," Mattie said.

"The workmanship is sound," Thomas said by way of a compliment.

Eyeing the brushes and the buckets in the corner, Mattie set Kathleen down. "Alice said everything I need would be right here." She looked at the supplies and turned to Thomas, confused. "I don't see any paint anywhere."

Thomas pointed to a bag of lime. "To paint a building as large as this would cost far too much. Whitewash will have to do for now."

"Whitewash?" Mattie looked at the large burlap bag. "What am I supposed to do with this?"

"You mix it with water to make whitewash," Thomas told her. "Haven't you ever whitewashed anything?"

"No. Not exactly. Of course I know what whitewash is and I've seen it being used but I've never actually whitewashed anything. Or painted anything either," she confessed.

Thomas sighed. "You need water."

Mattie smiled and held out the large empty pail. "I think you'll have to use the pump near the general store. I'll put my apron on and get Kathleen settled down on a blanket with some toys."

"I don't intend to spend all morning carrying buckets of water up and down the road," he told her, annoyed.

"It's one bucket of water." She held out the pail again. He snatched it and stalked down the road. When he returned Mattie greeted him at the door. "Now, how much lime do I mix in with the water?"

Thomas sighed louder this time and stomped over to the bag of lime, the bucket of water in hand. Ripping it open, he added fistfuls of the powder until it reached the right consistency. Mattie took a clean brush, dipped it in the bucket then painted a streak on the wall. Puzzled, she turned to Thomas.

"There must be something wrong, Thomas. It's clear," she said.

"It doesn't turn white until it dries. That's what makes this a horrible job. You can't see where you've painted until it starts to dry and then you see all of the uneven brush strokes," he told her.

"You seem like you have experience whitewashing," Mattie said, trying to brush the liquid on the walls evenly.

"My brother and I wasted many beautiful spring days whitewashing the barn and all of the outbuildings. If it weren't for the threat of a good hiding from my father we'd have quit five minutes after we started," Thomas replied.

"I can't threaten you with a hiding." She held out a brush. "But I'd really like it if you helped me."

Frowning, he took the brush from her hand. They worked steadily in complete silence throughout the morning and the task went by quickly. By noon only one wall remained to be whitewashed.

Mattie pulled the ladder over into the corner. "I brought some food. We can eat after we're done this wall."

"As long as it's not those damn cabbage rolls you made for dinner last night," he answered with a small smile.

Mattie laughed. She climbed the ladder and painted several long strokes before stepping down a rung. Her skirts wrapped themselves around her legs, throwing her off-balance. She fell backward and Thomas quickly reached for her as she fell. He caught her by the waist but the force of the fall knocked them both to the floor. They landed in a heap facing each other, arms and legs intertwined, her head on his chest and his knee across her hip. For several seconds they both lay there breathing deeply,

"Are you hurt?" Mattie asked Thomas.

"No." He groaned and rolled onto his back. He rubbed his hip. "Are you?"

Mattie sat up and shook her head. "You broke my fall." She braced a hand on the floor and stood. Seeing Thomas struggle to bend his bad knee, Mattie held out a hand. He waved it away impatiently. Annoyed, Mattie crossed her arms and watched Thomas falter several more times.

"Oh, for goodness sake! Stop being so foolish!" Mattie grasped his left hand and pulled him to his feet.

"Woman, I told you I can get up by myself," Thomas yelled angrily.

"And I told you not to call me woman so I guess neither of us listens very well," Mattie retorted. She stopped and peered closely at Thomas' hair. Chuckling, she broke into a wide smile. "Your hair is full of sawdust."

Thomas brushed his hair with his hands and gestured to Mattie's skirt. "It's all over you too."

She looked down at a swathe of light-colored dust clinging to her dark skirt. Sighing, she gave her skirt a shake several times before noticing a patch of sawdust on her sleeve. Turning around as far as she could, she checked the back of her skirt. "I'm covered in it." She looked up and examined Thomas. "It's all over you too."

"Clothes can be washed," Thomas said dismissively as he picked up the fallen ladder and put a paintbrush back into the pail of whitewash.

"It looks like we've been rolling around on the floor.

Together," Mattie clarified. Grimacing, Mattie scratched her head roughly. "It's in my hair and it's itchy." She continued scratching and her hair tumbled loose from its plait.

Thomas held out her paintbrush. "There's no one around to see."

"I think I've even got sawdust on my neck." Mattie gathered her hair and twisted it up into a high bun, revealing the nape of her neck. She turned her back to Thomas. "Do you see anything?"

Thomas moved closer. Reaching out, he slowly ran a hand down Mattie's neck. Mattie reacted with a sharp intake of breath. She bit her lip and spun around. His senses heightened, Thomas brushed her lips lightly with his before deeply, roughly capturing her mouth. Mattie kissed him back hungrily. Her hands moved to his hair and she felt the pull of her body to his.

Breaking from her, Thomas rested his forehead on hers. The sound of their ragged, shallows breaths filled the room. Seconds passed, then minutes.

"We want different things, Mattie," he said hoarsely.

Mattie traced the scar that ran along his jaw. "I know," she told him.

He swallowed hard and let her go. "I have some supplies to buy. I'll be outside the general store when you're ready to go."

Mattie watched him leave, his kiss still smoldering on her lips.

CHAPTER EIGHTEEN

On Saturday morning Thomas mumbled that he was too busy to take Mattie shopping and that he'd arranged for the Taylors to take her to town on their way. It was the most he'd spoken to her since the day before at the church. Mattie nodded a stiff reply. The days that followed passed just as dismally. Thomas no longer came in for the noon meal. Mattie assumed he was eating by himself in Johnny's cabin or perhaps not at all. He came in briefly during dinner time but kept his head down, barely acknowledging her or Kathleen. He left as abruptly as he entered.

On Tuesday, Mattie peeked around the side of the house to see Dora Bradshaw arriving on a dappled grey mare. Dora waved and Mattie propped the spade she'd been using in the vegetable garden against the house.

Overjoyed at the prospect of having a real conversation with an adult instead of exchanging brief pleasantries, one-word answers and grunts, Mattie ran to greet her. "Dora, I'm so glad to see you."

"I needed to talk to you and I didn't want to wait," she said.

"Please, come up on the porch and sit down. Would you like some tea?" Mattie asked.

"Tea would be lovely but what I really want is a chance to hold that beautiful little girl," Dora said.

"She's having a nap but she should be up soon," Mattie told her. She went inside and set the water to boil. Taking off her apron, she went back out to the porch and sat down on the chair facing Dora.

"I have some news. It's good news, I hope," Dora told her. Mattie leaned forward expectantly. "Instead of writing a letter, I sent a telegram to my cousin in Chicago and she answered almost immediately. She's found you a position as a lady's companion. That is, if you're still interested."

Mattie nodded slowly. "That's wonderful. Thank you so much. Of course I'm still interested."

"Are you sure?" Dora asked gently. "Maybe you should wait for another position, until you're really sure this is the best thing to do. I haven't heard from some friends in Saint Louis. Maybe you should wait until they…"

Mattie cut her off. "No. It's best that I go now." She looked at Dora and wiped the tears from her eyes. "I have to go now."

Dora put a hand on her arm. "You're smart enough to know your own mind, I reckon. You'll have to leave in two weeks' time. They'll be a ticket waiting for you at the station. For what it's worth, I think you're making a mistake."

"I need to do this," Mattie said.

"What do you need to do?" Thomas' voice boomed from behind her.

Mattie hastily wiped her tears with the back of her hand and turned to face him, a wide smile pasted on her face. "Dora was kind enough to find a position for me as a lady's companion. In Chicago. I leave in two weeks."

Shock passed over Thomas' face but as quickly as it appeared it disappeared again only to be replaced by a blank expression. "You decided not to stay in Boxwood and find yourself a husband here?" he asked dully.

"I think I will find more opportunities in a big city like Chicago," Mattie told him.

"As I said before, life out here is hard. It's not really a place for a woman used to a life in New York City. You've made the right decision." He turned to Dora. "I sure could use your help finding a family to take in the baby.

"You're not going to keep Kathleen here with you?" Mattie asked, shocked that he would be so willing to break the bond he'd made with his daughter.

"I have a cattle ranch to run and you know that I don't know the first thing about raising a child. It's the best solution for everyone," he said.

"It seems we've both found the best solution for everyone," Mattie said sadly.

Thomas turned on his heel and stomped off of the porch, pausing on the third stair for a few seconds. Glancing back slightly, it seemed as though he wanted to say something. Instead, he adjusted his hat and continued past the barnyard and out into the north field.

It was best, Thomas reminded himself as he surveyed his small herd of cattle lazing in the afternoon sun. She was a good woman; she would move on and find herself a good man. That's what he wanted to tell her before he walked away but couldn't. He was too afraid Mattie would be able to see through his lie, that something in his eyes would betray his secret: he wanted desperately to be a good man, a man who was good enough for her.

Now that the baby was well he didn't need her anymore. She came here looking for a husband and she certainly wasn't going to find one living in his house and looking after his daughter. She had a plan and she'd best follow the plan. It was only temporary. All of these thoughts came into his head, rolling through his brain at lightning speed, all of them logical reasons why Mattie should leave. And still... she seemed to fit so well into life in Boxwood, into *his* life.

All of those logical reasons, Thomas realized with a sudden start, were just excuses he'd made up so that he didn't have to risk anything. Self pity, misery and disappointment, he realized, had become so comfortable he wore them like an old coat. They felt good wrapped around him because they turned everyone away. He didn't need to put any effort into his life beyond breathing; nobody expected anything from him. He tried to lay the blame for his torment everywhere; his father, the war, his wounds, his troubled marriage, even his daughter. He had tried to lay blame everywhere except squarely where it belonged: on his shoulders. And now it was too late.

Chapter Nineteen

Every encounter with Thomas, though they were minimal, was fraught with tension to the point where Mattie was sure she might lose her mind. So much so that when Alice stopped in and asked if she wanted to accompany her to town, Mattie jumped at the chance. She took Kathleen, packed a few supplies and climbed onto the wagon seat without advising Thomas where she was going.

"We'll stop at the general store first, if you don't mind," Alice said as she guided the wagon into a spot outside the livery.

"That's perfect. I have to pick up a few supplies for my trip," Mattie answered.

Alice sighed. "I wish you'd reconsider. Just write the old lady and tell her you're not coming. Or send a telegram; it'll be faster. You can live with Will and I. Or take a room at the hotel. Or we can find a handsome, dashing man who wants to get married. Anything. Just please don't go."

Mattie smiled at her friend's dramatics. "I can't stay."

Alice hugged her fiercely. "I'm going to miss you."

Mattie hugged her back just as hard. "And I'll miss you but I promise to write and tell you all about Chicago. And you must write to me and tell me all of the news from Boxwood."

"That won't even fill a page," Alice groaned.

The women climbed down from the wagon and after carefully placing Kathleen in the sling, they walked across the rough dirt street and onto the sidewalk. As they passed the telegraph office Joshua waved, beckoning them inside.

Bells jingled as the door swung open. "Good morning, Joshua," Mattie said.

"Good morning. You're just the lady I wanted to see," he replied. "I received a telegram for you from your friend Rose late yesterday evening."

"I knew she'd come through!" Mattie said. "What did she say?"

Joshua searched through a pile of papers on his desk until he found what he was looking for. "Augustus Hendricks wanted in several jurisdictions including New York and Philadelphia. Fraudulent land deals. Story in major newspapers months ago. Advise caution and contact authorities. Rose," he read.

"I knew his name sounded familiar!" Mattie said.

"We need to tell Sheriff Bradshaw," Alice insisted.

Mattie turned to Joshua. "We need more information. Does anyone in Boxwood subscribe to newspapers from out east? Or even a Chicago newspaper? They may have carried the story."

Joshua shook his head. "Sorry, Mattie. Not that I know of."

"Wait a second," Alice said. "I bought a hat a few months ago at the general store and it came wrapped in newspaper."

"The Telfords get all of those goods from out east," Joshua added.

"Joshua, you go find the Sheriff. Alice, let's go to the general store and see if they have any pages from a New York or Philadelphia newspaper," Mattie said.

As the women hurried down the boardwalk, Mattie tried to make sense of this new information. What was Hendricks up to and why was he targeting Thomas?

They burst into the general store, causing Mrs. Telford to look up from her ledger. "Good morning Miss Robinson and Mrs. Taylor."

"Good morning, Mrs. Telford," Mattie said, hurriedly. "This may seem like an odd request but we desperately need to look through all of the newspapers your hats and clothes are wrapped in. We're looking for a particular news story and it's very important."

Mrs. Telford set down her pen. "This way." She marched to the curtain that divided the store and storeroom and, drawing it aside, motioned for Alice and Mattie to follow her. She pointed to a neatly organized corner. "All of the hats are on the shelf in individual boxes. The clothing is still in the trunks."

"Thank you so much," Mattie hugged her quickly.

Taken back, Mrs. Telford adjusted her glasses. "You're welcome dear. Just don't make a mess," she said sternly.

"I'll look through the clothing," Alice offered, pulling up a stool.

Mattie took down a hatbox and opened it. She checked the newspaper tucked around the hat. "This is a New York paper."

Alice held up a torn strip of newspaper. "So is this."

Silently, the pair worked unwrapping newspaper and scanning it for any sign of Hendrick's name. After half an hour Alice stretched and rubbed her back. "I've checked through both trunks and there's nothing."

Mattie sighed. "Nothing in the hat boxes either. It was worth a try. I just hope the Sheriff can telegraph the authorities in New York or Chicago and get a reply back in time to arrest Hendricks before he leaves town."

Alice stood and leaned against a shelf of new shoes. She picked up a dainty pair with tiny little black leather buttons and a heel. "Aren't these beautiful?" she gushed. She held them up and examined them from every angle. "They're darling but Mrs. Telford will never sell them. They're ridiculously impractical for life in the Dakota Territory."

Mattie reached her hand into the toe of the shoe and smiled at Alice. "They could be useful after all." She withdrew a ball of newspaper. Unrolling it, she smoothed the paper down on the floor. "Alice! Look!" she exclaimed.

Pointing to a long paragraph on the left side of the paper, Mattie read excitedly. "A warrant for the arrest of Augustus Hendricks was sworn today in New York Superior court. Mr. Hendricks is already wanted for fraud in Georgia, Philadelphia, Boston and Baltimore. He sometimes goes by the name of Gus Henderson, Henry Augustus and Lionel Hendricks. He is believed to be in the company of a man known as Lee Beauregard who often poses as a lawyer. Mr. Hendricks has been tried and found guilty of forging deeds, land documents and loan agreements in order to obtain property fraudulently which he then sells to unsuspecting individuals and companies. He was last seen in Cincinnati where he fraudulently obtained a large estate occupied by the sisters of Our Lady of Assumption. It is believed that he is headed west."

Joshua stepped through the curtain. "Sheriff Bradshaw is at a farm about twenty miles west of town. Dora expects him home today but she doesn't know when."

Mattie folded up the newspaper page and slipped it into her reticule. "We need to get Thomas."

"Will is going to be furious with me but I'm not keeping the horses at a walk," Alice told Mattie as they hurried back to the livery.

Arriving back at the ranch in record time, the women found Thomas in the barn cleaning out stalls. The expression on Mattie's face caused him to abandon the pitchfork in the stall and hurry toward them. "Is it Kathleen? Has something happened to her?"

Mattie handed him the newspaper story. "It's Hendricks."

After reading the story Thomas insisted on returning to town immediately. Despite his protests, Mattie would not be left behind. Leaving Kathleen snuggled and asleep in Alice's arms, Mattie and Thomas hitched the horses to the wagon and returned to Boxwood.

"I just can't figure it out," Mattie said, shaking her head. "What does Hendricks want with your farm? It's a beautiful farm," she assured Thomas "but why is he so determined to get it?"

"Mine and Johnny's," Thomas corrected her. "He's determined to get my land and Johnny's too."

Mattie thought for a minute. "Maybe that's what he's after," she mused.

"What?" he asked.

"Maybe he has to have both pieces of land," she suggested. "Maybe whatever he's planning will only work if he has both ranches."

"The only thing both parcels of land have in common other than decent soil is the river," he said.

Entering Boxwood, Thomas guided the horses down the main street. He passed the livery and stopped in front of the hotel. He was inside less than two minutes before returning to the wagon. He continued to the end of the main street and turned left down a short road until he came to a large area that was home to a disorganized collection of lean-tos, tents and wagons. Men were gathered around open fires laughing and drinking while food cooked in large pots. Discarded garbage, scraps and liquor bottles littered the thick mud.

"A shantytown?" Mattie asked. "If Hendricks is so wealthy he can lend money why isn't he staying at the hotel?"

"He got kicked out of the hotel for not paying. The clerk told me last he heard Hendricks was staying in a lean-to rented out by Mrs. Andersson." He pointed to a shack with a green door. "That one's hers."

Mattie climbed down from the wagon and looked around. "The window's open. He would have heard us approach. It doesn't look like he's here."

WIFE NOT REQUIRED

"I'm going to look around," Thomas said.

Mattie followed him up the ragged dirt path to the front door.

"Maybe you should go and see if the Sheriff's back yet," Thomas suggested.

"And I suppose I should just run across town? I can't drive the wagon. Besides, you're not leaving me behind. I'm coming in too," Mattie answered.

The door swung open stiffly. Thomas glanced around the small room. "He's not here."

Mattie stepped inside on the dirt floor. She reached out and pulled the ragged quilt from the cot. "He must have papers hidden somewhere in here."

"You don't think I'd be so stupid as to leave incriminating evidence just laying around, do you?" Hendricks entered the room behind them and shut the door.

"The Sheriff knows all about you," Mattie told him.

"I doubt that. He's out of town at the moment and by the time he returns I'll be gone," Hendricks told her.

"What do you want?" Thomas asked.

"I have everything I came for. My associate is in Fort Laramie registering your land to me. And Johnny's farm too, as a matter of fact," Hendricks said jovially. "Don't worry, Tom. I'm not a monster. You can't stay in your house until winter. I won't even charge you rent."

"That farm is mine!" Thomas shouted. "I have until September to pay my loan."

Hendricks shook his head in mock sadness. "I'm afraid not. No, see you missed three payments in a row. I have to terminate our agreement and I'm authorized to take the farm as payment."

"I've never missed a payment and you know it," Thomas hissed.

"I have paperwork that says otherwise. I can't show it to you; it's on its way to Fort Laramie along with the deed to your land that you signed over to me," Hendricks said.

"Once the land registry office discovers what you've done, they'll give Thomas back his land," Mattie said.

"Oh, they may. But that hardly matters to me because by tomorrow night the farms will be sold to a company and they'll no longer be my problem. Some group of eastern fools wants to start a large-scale farming operation, if you can imagine. Bonanza farming, they call it. They wanted a thousand acres with access to water so I provided. You can fight them and their lawyers for your land."

"Johnny's place and mine only add up to four hundred acres," Thomas said.

"That's all I could get my hands on this quickly but once those easterners dam the river and block off access to the water all the farms downriver will be worthless. I'm sure they'll pick them up for pennies. At least, that's what I told them," Hendricks laughed.

"The Taylors and all of your neighbors, Thomas!" Mattie said. "They'll be ruined."

"No," Thomas said definitively. "You can't do this."

"I already have," Hendricks said. He pushed past Thomas and stooped, pulling a large suitcase out from under the bed. "Excuse me. I'm on my way out of town. Miss Robinson, you're a lovely woman. For a Yankee." He touched his hat and bowed slightly.

Thomas stepped in front of Hendricks. "You're staying until the Sheriff comes."

Hendricks smiled coldly. "I don't think so." From under the mattress he pulled a heavy iron pipe. "This isn't the first time I've had to leave town quickly."

Thomas advanced to grab the bar from his hands and Hendricks swung it viciously, catching Thomas on his sore arm.

"I got hit worse than that standing in line for water at the prison camp," he said through clenched teeth.

Hendricks swung again and struck Thomas' left knee, sending him down on the dirt floor.

"Thomas!" Mattie cried out.

"Stay back," Hendricks threatened, the pipe in the air.

"Mattie," Thomas cried out as he rocked in pain.

Mattie backed up against the squat little stove across from the door. Hendricks smirked and picked up his suitcase. Sensing his opportunity at catching Hendricks off guard, Thomas lunged at him. He pulled him down but Hendricks was quicker and swung the heavy suitcase at his head. It connected and Thomas fell backward stunned. Hendricks got to his feet, picked up the suitcase and headed for the door.

Grasping at the edge of the stove, Mattie's hand felt the heavy iron handle of a frying pan. As Hendricks turned and reached the door, she grabbed the pan with both hands and crossed the room. She swung and connected with Hendrick's shoulder. He cried out in pain and turned. She swung again and hit him on the side of his head, alongside his ear. His legs crumpled underneath him and he slumped down to the ground. Mattie dropped the pan and ran to Thomas.

"Are you alright?" she asked, rigorously examining his head for wounds.

"I'm fine. He just stunned me," Thomas said, shooing her hands away from him.

"Langley, you in there?" a voice called from outside.

Hendrick's round body blocked Mattie's path to the door so she grabbed his arms up over his head and dragged him to the middle of the room. He moaned but remained unconscious. Mattie opened the door and waved the Sheriff and his deputy inside.

Seeing Hendricks laying on the floor, the Sheriff nodded to his deputy. "Get him up and over to the jail. Better send someone for Granny White so she can tend to that head wound." He examined Hendricks and looked at Thomas. "You do that with a fist?"

Thomas gestured a thumb to Mattie. "With a frying pan," he said.

Sheriff Bradshaw laughed. "Well, you are really something! Johnny Stark was right about you after all."

Mattie looked at the Sheriff, confused. "What do you mean?"

"I've just come from the abandoned Claridge farm outside of town. Two bounty hunters had Hendrick's partner cornered in the barn there. We got him and he had all the paperwork with him. Looks like he was heading to Fort Laramie to register a bunch of forged deeds, including a forged deed for your property, Langley. We found the original deed for Johnny's place along with a letter the old man wrote last winter. Hendricks must have found it when he broke into the cabin to steal the deed." Sheriff Bradshaw reached into his pocket and pulled out a folded piece of paper. He handed it to Mattie.

Mattie unfolded it and skimmed through it. A look of astonishment crossed over her face and she shook her head. "I don't understand. This has my name on it." She kept reading. "It says that if Mr. Stark dies his farm is mine."

"Johnny must have known that he didn't have a lot of time left. He knew you were coming so he made sure that if anything happened the farm would be yours. There's also a tidy little sum of money from his time in the army," the Sheriff told her.

"But he didn't even know me," Mattie said softly.

"I guess the fact that you were willing to come all this way just to marry him, to make sure he wasn't alone in his old age, meant something to him," Sheriff Bradshaw said.

"It's mine, then? The farm? The money?" Mattie asked.

"The whole two hundred acres," the Sheriff replied.

Mattie looked up and saw Thomas staring at her. This didn't change anything. In fact, it only hardened her resolve to leave. She couldn't stay and live on the farm next to Thomas. She walked slowly across the room to him. "I didn't know John Stark but you did. It must have been a great comfort to him in his final days to look out of his cabin and see your house across the river and know that he didn't have to die alone on the land. You might have thought he was a fool for bringing me here but you were a good friend to him." She took Thomas' hand and placed the paper in it. "The farm is yours to do with as you please. You deserve it, Thomas. You're a good man and a good father to Kathleen."

"I can't take it," Thomas mumbled. "I don't want it. You need it."

Mattie shook her head and smiled broadly, tears tracing a path down her face. "What do I need of a farm in the

Dakota Territory? I leave for Chicago tomorrow after the boxed lunch social."

"You're still planning to go?" the Sheriff asked, incredulous.

Looking at Thomas, Mattie answered, "Arrangements have been made."

CHAPTER TWENTY

Mattie placed another boxed lunch on the long table made of boards and fluffed up the blue ribbon.

"That one's Clara's, isn't it?" Alice said, coming up behind her.

"How do you know?" Mattie turned around, surprised. "And you shouldn't say it so loudly in case someone hears. These lunches are supposed to be surprises until they're purchased."

"Oh, everybody knows that's Clara's. Including Joshua, I imagine. He gave her that cameo she always wears on a blue ribbon," Alice said. From a basket on her arm she took out a box wrapped in yellow fabric. "Here's mine."

"Will didn't see it, did he? It's supposed to be a surprise," Mattie said.

"I wrapped it up in some of the fabric I had leftover from making baby clothes," Alice touched her growing stomach. "I'm sure he wasn't paying attention to my sewing."

"Everyone looks like they're having so much fun," Mattie said happily.

"Where's your lunch?" Alice asked.

"It's the brown basket with the gold ribbon," Mattie gestured to the table. Seeing her friend smirk, Mattie crossed her arms, pretending to be angry. "Don't worry. Dora helped me with the biscuits."

Alice laughed and then her face turned serious and sad. She hugged her. "I noticed your trunk in the back of the Bradshaw's wagon."

"My train leaves today after the social," Mattie said. She took and deep breath and forced the tears away. "I thought it was better that they brought me today. Thomas wasn't coming anyway and I didn't want him to make a special trip into town just for me. Plus, I think it was easier to say goodbye to Kathleen this way." It was no use. She couldn't hold back her tears any longer and they flowed down her cheeks.

Alice searched through her reticule and handed Mattie a handkerchief. Mattie blotted her eyes.

"Don't cry," Alice said sternly. "Or you'll make me cry too. I cry at the drop of a hat these days. Let's just enjoy your last day in Boxwood without any tears."

"I will if you will," Mattie promised.

Dora Bradshaw walked up to the pair. "Everything looks wonderful," she told them.

"Thank you," Mattie said. "I just hope we can raise some money for the hall."

Dora looked around. "Well, the whole town seems to have turned out. We have fifty-three boxed lunches on the table ready to be sold."

Mattie looked, incredulous. "Fifty-three? I didn't know there were fifty-three women in the county, let alone in the town."

"Absolutely everybody wanted to participate. Granny White made a lunch and so did Josiah Sittler's four little girls," Dora said.

Alice laughed. "I saw that. Josiah won't have any trouble figuring out which four lunches to buy. They wrapped all of them with exactly the same fabric."

Mr. MacDougall called for everyone's attention. "I'm so happy we could all gather together in our new hall. Some offered their time, others offered their money, some offered both to build this place, a place where we can all come together as a town. As the founder of Boxwood, it means a great deal to me. As you can see, though, we're not quite done. We need to buy a new window before the cold sets in and the lumber for the benches still needs to be paid for. A committee of ladies has organized this event to help us with those costs. I'd like to introduce Miss Robinson, who came up with this idea in the first place, to explain how this is going to work. Miss Robinson?"

Mattie nodded stepped forward. "We have some beautiful baskets here, no doubt containing delicious lunches. We want to do this in an orderly fashion." The crowd laughed. "Mrs. Taylor will hold up each of the baskets one at a time and I will ask for buyers. If two or more gentlemen want the same lunch basket they will have to bid on it. The highest bid takes it and gets to lunch with the lady who made it. The purchase price of each basket will start at two bits. Once you've made the purchase hold up your basket and your lunch companion will find you. Mrs. Taylor, let's see the first basket, please."

Alice held up a basket decorated with fresh wildflowers. Sheriff Bradshaw held up a hand. "I'll take that one."

Dora looked at him. "Are you sure?" she asked carefully.

He smiled proudly. "Absolutely!"

Dora pinched her lips in a straight line. "You hate wildflowers. They make you sneeze."

"I'm willing to risk it," the Sheriff said. He handed Alice the coins and took the basket.

"That's mine!" Granny White yelled from the crowd. "The Sheriff chose my basket!" She hurried over to his side.

"Indeed he did," Dora said tightly.

The Sheriff reached into his pocket and pulled out two

more coins. "I'll also take the box with the red bow since I'm pretty sure there's a nice blueberry pie in that one."

Dora laughed. "You're an impossible man!"

"And how do you know what is in it?" Mattie asked playfully. "It's supposed to be a surprise!"

Dora smiled. "I may have hinted."

"If the one with the red bow has one of Dora's blueberry pies in it, then I want that one. I'll pay four bits!" yelled a man at the back of the crowd.

"I'm not willing to let that pie go," the Sheriff told him. "I'll pay a dollar."

The crowd clapped and the man at the back shrugged good-naturedly. Alice handed over the basket to the Sheriff and he walked away, Dora on one arm and Granny White on the other.

Alice held up the next basket. "This beautiful basket with the blue ribbon is pretty heavy." She took a sniff. "I think I smell fresh bread and chocolate cake."

"I'll take that one," Joshua called out.

"That's mine!" Clara squealed excitedly.

"You two enjoy your lunch," Mattie said as she took Joshua's money.

The basket belonging to Josiah Sittler's eldest daughter was auctioned next. Josiah bid first and, much to his surprise, a hand went up in the air and a quiet voice called out a bid of four bits. A young man, red in the face but grinning ear to ear came forward to claim his basket. Several more baskets were auctioned before Alice held up Mattie's basket decorated with gold ribbon.

Evan Wilmont held up his hand. "I want that one."

"Four bits over here," yelled an older man dressed in a plain cotton shirt and blue trousers.

"A dollar," Evan countered.

"A dollar and a half," said another young man.

"A dollar and six bits," Evan said, reluctantly.

"Two dollars," offered the older man.

"Three dollars," boomed a loud voice near the door.

Mattie looked up. "Thomas!" she said in surprise. She stepped off of the stage and hurried to his side. "What are you doing here? Is Kathleen alright?"

"She's fine. Mrs. Telford has her," he gestured to the older woman standing by the door with Kathleen.

"Three and a half," Evan said loudly.

Approaching Evan, Thomas straightened to his full six feet and seven inches. "I came for that lunch basket." The crowd grew quiet, unsure if Thomas intended to start a fight with the younger man. Instead, he leaned forward and spoke very softly. "Please, let me buy it."

"Mr. Langley, the last bid was three and a half. Can you do better than that?" Alice said from the stage.

"I'll go as high as four," Thomas told her.

Dora slapped Evan on the back. "I'd let it go. The lunch isn't that good, except for the biscuits."

Evan nodded and Thomas stuck out his hand. After a brief handshake, Evan backed away into the crowded hall.

"The lunch is yours, Mr. Langley," Alice said, lifting up the basket.

Thomas took it and with Mattie on his arm, walked over to Mrs. Telford. Mattie gathered Kathleen into her arms and the baby gurgled happily and clutched Mattie's hair.

"You were very kind to Evan," Mattie told him.

He set the basket down and clasped her hand. "Don't go."

"Thomas, if you're here because you're afraid you won't find someone to look after Kathleen," she began.

He shook his head. "Don't go to Chicago. Stay in Boxwood. With me and Kathleen."

Mattie stopped jostling the baby up and down in her arms and looked into his eyes. "What are you saying?"

"I'm not the kind of man who's good with words, Mattie. I don't know how to say it any other way than plain. You're like no one I've ever met before. You're not afraid of anything, including me. You're smart and beautiful, even though you don't see it. I don't know how to be a good husband or even a good man but I want to try. With you. I was thinking that maybe I could stay at Johnny's place and you could stay in the house. I could court you proper, the way a woman like you deserves to be courted. And if, after some time, you decided you wanted to leave I'd respect that."

"And if I wanted to stay?" Mattie asked.

"I'd ask you to marry me, woman!" Thomas answered.

"Oh, for pity's sake just kiss her," Dora yelled from the table across the room where she was eating with the Sheriff and Granny White.

Mattie giggled and Thomas slid an arm around her waist, pulling her in closer. They both moved toward each other and kissed slowly and gently, Kathleen snuggled in between them.

68010382R00109

Made in the USA
Columbia, SC
03 August 2019